Trans*(____).

We Won't Be Erased!

An anthology of poems and song lyrics by transgender and non-binary writers

Edited by Dr Ash Brockwell

First published 2019 by Reconnecting Rainbows Press

Printed by Lightning Source International via CompletelyNovel

www.completelynovel.com

ISBN 978-1-7872-3409-3

To that person who needed to read this today
(you know who you are):

You are enough.
You are valid.
You are loved.

INTRODUCTION

Ash Brockwell PhD FRSA

The idea for this book was born out of the frustration of trying to express myself through abstract art. I'd been offered the chance to have a solo exhibition of paintings at The Art House, Southampton, during Pride season, and planning it a year in advance gave me the chance to think carefully about what the show would communicate. I wanted it to be deeply personal, almost autobiographical, and reflect the issues that had been playing on my mind for years: gender, identities, mental health, hate crime, media bias against trans and non-binary people, and the need to reconnect with nature and rebuild community. But as I started making new work for the exhibition, one thing troubled me: the fear that nobody would 'get the point', which is probably an occupational hazard for all abstract painters. It got worse when even my nearest and dearest responded to my works-in-progress with a puzzled expression and a vague nod.

Part of me kept insisting that it didn't matter, and that everyone sees something different in an abstract painting anyway – depending on who they are, where they are, and what they've experienced. Arguably, there's no 'right answer' when it comes to the interpretation of art, and everyone's individual ways of understanding an image are valid and meaningful. But there was also a part of me, irritated with the constant misgendering and deadnaming of early transition (being referred to with the wrong pronouns and the wrong name, respectively) that wanted to scream out, 'Don't you see? THIS is the point I was trying to make!' A possible solution revealed itself when a poem popped into my head uninvited, inspired by a line from T. S. Eliot's poem *The Love Song of J. Alfred Prufrock:* '*That is not what I meant at all. That is not it, at all.*'

A ~~thousand words~~ 227 words

A picture can be worth a thousand words, they say;

What happens when that picture gets misunderstood?

You really can't deny you'll see it your own way:

You'll never see it through MY eyes. You never could.

Your thousand words might say the opposite of mine,

I simply can't assume you'll know my true intent...

You might think, 'Swastika!' when viewing my design;

Like Prufrock, I would wail, 'That isn't what I meant!'

What you see is what you get? Well, yes, or so I've read;

For people such as me, that may not be the case.

While staring at an M, you see an F instead!

Identity is more, I'm sure, than voice-meets-face.

Shapeshifters like ourselves can never quite rely

on standard visual cues to show you who we are:

But words can miss the mark as well, for all we try,

And every failed pronoun leaves its subtle scar.

So... can I find a way to help you understand?

Could words, perhaps, succeed where images might fail?

Or what about the two together, hand in hand -

A thousand words, or less, to tell each picture's tale?

I'll let the haters hate, and cry, 'It isn't art!'

When images and words unite, and share a wall:

If anything I do can soothe an aching heart,

I've nothing left to lose. This closet is too small.

Fast-forward a few months and I had a growing collection of poems - and so did my wife, Kay. By the time Trans Day of Visibility came around in March 2019, we both got brave enough to read some on stage at the 'Moving Voices' open mic night, organised as part of the Art SO Trans event in Southampton. At the event, we met other trans and non-binary poets and songwriters, and the idea for an anthology was born.

I put out a call for contributions to trans support groups on Facebook, as well as reaching out directly to some of our mutual friends who were already posting their poetry on social media. I was keen to attract a mix of trans men, trans women and non-binary people, and to give a voice to trans people of colour, who are often at a higher risk of erasure because of the intersection of racism and transphobia. Five months later, the result was this collection: over 80 poems by 26 writers from the United Kingdom, Kenya and the USA.

There wasn't any competition or judgement involved in the submissions process – as trans people, we all have more than enough judgement in our lives already. My position is that every poem is valid and powerful in its own right, just as every trans person is valid and powerful in their own right and shouldn't be compared to anyone else. In this book, you'll find the whole spectrum of experience and professionalism, from teenagers writing their first poems to established performers.

Inevitably, some of the poems in this collection will resonate with you more than others. Some will make you laugh, some will make you cry, some will make you fume, and some might leave you thinking, 'I'd probably have done that differently'. But we are who we are, and our words are our authentic words, uncensored and unfiltered: that's the whole point.

This collection matters because it's been an extremely difficult year for trans people in the UK and USA, in terms of media representation: even newspapers that are usually sympathetic to diversity seem to have been led astray by lies and misconceptions. Through an increasingly well-funded and organised anti-trans campaign, trans women are being portrayed as perverted men who want to invade women's spaces, from toilets and refuges to professional sport.

Trans men, when they're mentioned at all – which is rare - are presented as misguided young women, brainwashed into self-mutilation by a dangerous cult of 'transactivists'. Meanwhile, the existence of non-binary people is barely acknowledged at all. Two of my poems (*Transactivist* and *Sometimes Waving but Mostly Drowning*) directly express this frustration with the media portrayal of trans issues, and several other poems in the collection hint at it in different ways.

What I'd love to convey with this book is not only that #TransMenAreMen, #TransWomenAreWomen and #NonBinaryIsValid, but also more broadly that all #TransPeopleArePeople. We might all care about different things, and write about them in different ways, but in the end we're all as human as anyone else.

In the same way as no cis person would want to be remembered as 'just a man' or 'just a woman', there's more to us than our gender, as one of the chapter titles points out. Trans people are writers and artists, parents and children, siblings and niblings, friends and lovers, support workers and teachers, software engineers and students, priests and entrepreneurs, musicians and health professionals, and so much more besides. Our transness, our dysphoria and our experiences of prejudice and discrimination don't consume our whole lives.

Sharing poetry is an act of vulnerability: we put our innermost thoughts and feelings, things we wouldn't normally bring up in everyday conversation, out there in the public domain for everyone to read.

As trans people, we're opening ourselves up to scrutiny from a media that we fully expect to be hostile to our very existence. Why would anyone choose to do that? Why not stay in the chrysalis? As I highlight in the song *Coming Out Of My Chrysalis* on page 25 and the last two lines of '227 words' above, the craving for freedom of expression - powerful though it is - only gets us so far before it's swamped by fear. What actually gives us the final push to break out of the cocoon is the yearning to make a difference to someone else.

f you're trans or non-binary and still in the closet, or newly out, we hope you'll find a line or two in this book to reassure you that you're not alone and that there's nothing 'wrong' with what you're feeling.

If you're mid-transition (or even post-transition) and having a difficult time at the moment, we hope we can manage to convince you that things will get better.

If you're a member of the Organised Anti-Trans Brigade – an 'oatbie', as one of our wonderful contributors puts it – who's bought this book in the hope of finding something to attack us with, please be as creative with your insults as you possibly can. All negative feedback on this project will be collated and used in a new artwork entitled 'Don't Read the Comments', and if it's misspelled and ungrammatical, so much the better. Throw us your hate and we'll turn it into something positive, in the spirit of singers like Madilyn Bailey, Elise Ecklund, Colleen Ballinger, James Charles, Social Repose and Bethany Mota (on YouTube). For, as you'll read in my song *The Other Side of Darkness: 'on the other side of hatred, there's a Love that always wins.'*

And if you're an ally, we hope you'll find something that helps you to see beyond the media hype, understand our diverse community a little better, and support your trans friends and family. We are all in this together.

Profits from the sale of this book will be donated to **The Refugee Trans Initiative**, a project led by a Ugandan trans refugee woman called Vanilla and her Congolese boyfriend of five years. The couple run a safe house for trans and gender non-conforming refugees in Kenya, accommodating 12 people in a three-bedroom house. As Vanilla explains it, 'We have faced the worst possible abuse, from police arrest to torture and rejection from the community. We strive to live and have gone through the most painful process: it's a challenge every day, and even earning a living or getting a job is a problem. We have been relying on the mercy of well-wishers but now we've formed an initiative and a safe house for refugee trans people, where we do advocacy, activism and empowering trans refugees and the community at large. We look out for opportunities to empower our community. With your help, the lives of trans refugees can be saved."

Finding ourselves

The poems in this chapter are all about our identities as trans people – how we find, understand and create the 'selves' that we present to the world, as well as the ones that we choose to keep hidden. They reflect the challenges of navigating a world that, all too often, doesn't see us in the ways we see ourselves.

While different people vary in terms of what triggers dysphoria or post-traumatic stress, the poems in this chapter come with only the mildest of trigger warnings. They aren't violent, don't delve deeply into challenging themes of dysphoria or transphobia, and usually end on an upbeat note.

Challenge everything.

RKP

Because they don't understand it,

Doesn't mean you can't be it.

Life is a turn and a twist,

Of things unfathomable,

Of things too beautiful, they are unquantifiable,

But they are real.

Shaped by experience congealment,

Your identity is not up for argument.

Life is not just black and white,

We are different shades,

Who you are is not a debate,

De-bait the opening statement...

That this has to be this,

That this has to be that,

You can't be this,

You can't be that.

Challenge societies' cement.

Question the rules they are hell-bent

On making you bow and bend,

To my lovers, weirdos, and friends,

To those I'll never meet again,

You define your lines.

Growing on delicate spines,

Your faults, your whinges, your whines,

They result in your shine,

Be original, make this ''mine.''

But be kind,

Be loving,

Be respectful,

Show them your soul.

The only person you are, is you.

Remember unique is spelt with a ''U.''

Your 'AFAB' Does Not Erase Me*

Ash Brockwell

Brain: Male.

Heart: Male.

Soul: Male.

And yet you imagine a word

on a forty-year-old page

can invalidate all of these?

#GetALife #DailyFail

Yes, I was assigned-female-at-birth,

grew up behind net curtains with my secrets concealed inside,

where nobody (and least of all me)

understood quite what was denied.

I refused to answer to my given name at five,

hid growing curves under baggy sweaters at twelve,

felt weird and wrong around girls who wore make-up and heels

and spent their weekends shopping for pink lace bras:

that was all I knew. There were things that I never tried to do,

because it just wasn't 'done', within that net; and many things

that I didn't say, and couldn't have said, however I tried,

because the words weren't even invented yet.

There wasn't a language, then, for people like me.

#TransgenderBoy and #TransgenderMan were years away,

The teachers could have been fired just for saying 'gay'.

So, in conclusion: secrets: kept.

Yet your 'AFAB' cannot define me now.

#WontBeErased #WontBeDenied

My #ExistenceIsResistance;

and if you dare try to delete me, I WILL resist.

Assigning pink lace flowers to hide what you can't accept

can no more erase the blue core of a #TransMan like me

than King Canute's command 'Thus far, and no further'

could ever hold back the inrushing Solent tide. Whatever

you choose to call me, whatever you say, I will ride the waves

to places you never dreamed, and live my self-made life

as my truest self anyway.   There's no way in again, now I'm out.

Because this is who I am, and have always been,

and the only alternative is…

No.

Let's not go there.

I am here.

Defiantly turquoise.

Dynamic.

Impassioned.

Alive.

So take your eraser, take your net curtains, and go;

I am still here, no longer silent, at this meeting-place

of sea and shore, persistently pushing on as the waves do,

and reminding myself day after day that there are more

ways than one to be a man. There are more ways than one

for the deep essence of a human soul to survive.

* From 'TransVerse' exhibition, 2019:
www.ashbrockwell.com/transverse/afab

Outside Inside - a song

The Bleeding Obvious: http://bleedingobvious.uk/rainbowheart

I want to live outside how I feel on the inside.

But instead I'm on the outside looking in.

The life I live each day shouldn't define me

I should learn to take it on the chin.

But I'm tired of living life in the danger zone

When the mirror lies to me every single day.

I want to show outside what's on the inside.

Outside I'm on the inside looking through.

The things you say each day will not define me.

Come at it from a different point of view.

And I'm tired of living life in the danger zone

Where my head lies to me every single day.

One day I'll live outside what's on the inside.

For now I'm on the outside looking in.

The life I live each day does not define me.

And I need to be outside this skin, I'm in.

It's not easy being you, when you're hiding in plain view.

And life is questioned every single day.

Outside, inside.

Outside, inside.

Disorder

Kestral Gaian

There are times that the mind

needs to hide away.

Never telling the reason,

never quite back to stay.

In absence it spins you

great stories to say –

a boy who's connected,

a young girl's new day.

So you live out these stories,

that your mind leaves for you,

until it returns,

and starts life anew.

Misanthropic Same Space

Jon/Joan Knight

I have dates with Miss Ann Trophy,

I don't like her,

she doesn't like me,

That's all upon that we agree,

well that and fear of living free.

I moved her muscles against my will,

we have the bruises still.

Occupy the same space,

danger to selves and human race,

that glorious, gentle, sublime disgrace.

Maybe we will date again?

a pained pleasure, endured now and then.

Ann has dates with me there pencilled in,

we will meet and hope will win?

How to be a lady

Paula Adrianne

You learn it from mother

Your sister, or your aunt

But sometimes that's not possible

Sometimes you just can't

I watch the other ladies

I see how they behave

It's scary being a trainee girl

But I'm trying to be brave

I've had a fair few mistakes

I've often got it wrong

But I am a Yorkshire lass

And my spirit's very strong

I learnt how not to flash my knickers

When I climb out of cars

I learnt how to walk in heels

And how to fasten bras

I learned how to put make up on

So I don't look like a twat

How to wear a corset

So I don't look quite so fat

I've learnt not to fart in public

Pick my nose or swear

Learnt how to pluck my eyebrows

And how to dye my hair

I learned how to queue in toilets

When I have to pee

I've learned to stop pretending

I've learned to be just me.

Trans Priest

Bingo Allison

This stubble is a sacred

Powdered shadow of truth,

This hair is a holy

Fading pattern of youth,

These lips they are praying

Though the lipstick wore thin,

Brows bear the weight of the Christ Child

Like hefty St Christopher's limbs,

These shoulders are broad like an altar,

Rough like the texture of stone,

Breasts like the Holy Mother,

But lying more close to the bone,

Hips hard like the banks of the Jordan

Without the means to feel clean,

Thighs like edge of the Red Sea

Moses' staff planted firm in between.

A Holy Body shrouded in mystery

In firm foundation and blush,

With faltering step in Abraham's heels

I speak from my burning bush,

These dresses the robes of the preacher,

My saintly halo a tangled hairpiece,

Pout my ruby red lips as I deliver the Word,

Shake my hips as I call for the Peace.

The invisible will be visible,

Transitioned, and transformable.

Our lives are reformable.

All are reborn-able.

I will stand up and be seen,

Bright and new and clean,

Dysphoria released,

Your transgender priest.

Letter to a lost girl

Tyler Richins

I thought for weeks

I was never quite sure what to say.

I hear you all the time

You ask me if I remember our plan to be the first female president

To tell you the truth?

I don't

Many of my close friends know your name

None ever knew you

I never want to tell them what you were like

But at the same time

I do

I want to thank you

But at the same time i want to curse your name

Mia

It's your name that people first see on a job application

Mia

It's your name that teachers first see

Mia

It's your voice that people hear when I talk

It's your body they see

You're gone but

You are still the one everyone sees

It drives me crazy

I know how people don't want to see you go

But you're already gone

I bind your chest so I can walk without wanting to hide

Trying my best not to look like you

Your pictures are still on my profiles

When my dad looks at me he still sees you

All I want is for them to see Tyler

All they can see is Mia

I'm sorry

But no matter what, I never hated you.

Coming Out Of My Chrysalis – a song*

Ash Brockwell

I'm coming out of my chrysalis now,

I want to break out and touch the limitless sky,

For I've discovered my courage somehow:

See, I've been growing these wings,

and I think I might be ready to fly…

I'm coming out of my chrysalis now!

Here in the dark I've been transforming, growing my rainbow wings,

Now, with the sunlight's gentle warming,

see what the new day brings:

This is my moment, I'm deciding, this is my time to go…

All of the colours I've been hiding, I'm going to put on show!

I'm coming out of my chrysalis now…

But I never thought that it would take this long,

and I just don't know if I can be that strong,

Who'd have ever thought that coming out could hurt this way?

So, if it's not too late, I think I'll change my mind and stay…

No, I can't be me while I am stuck in here!

Got to find a way through all this doubt and fear,

Because from far away, I hear the flowers calling me,

And I realise how much they need me to be free…

Flowers, I hear you, just stay strong now, I will be with you soon.

Light's breaking through, it won't be long now…

tearing the thin cocoon…

I wasn't made to crawl forever, nettles are not my world,

One final push, it's now or never… See me with wings unfurled!

See, I've come out of my chrysalis now,

I've broken out now to touch the limitless sky,

For I discovered my courage somehow:

Just see these beautiful wings,

now I know at last I'm ready to fly!

Who needs that empty old chrysalis now?

* From 'TransVerse' exhibition, 2019:
www.ashbrockwell.com/transverse/out-of-the-chrysalis

Your pronoun. Question Mark.

RKP

They and their.

They and their.

They and their.

They and their.

They and their.

They and their.

Each time you say She, or her…

I'm reminded that I am not her daughter,

She'll never be a Mother,

But,

I am not your Sister,

Neither am I your Brother.

You'll all sit there, saying,

Be who you want to be,

Be happy,

Just 'B'.

My pronouns aren't heavy,

"I'm just so used to it."

But change exists for a reason.

"But you're not a thing."

I know… I am a person.

Who, doesn't feel seen,

I don't feel "there"…

Because hello, I'm standing right here.

I am neutral

A PH gender bender.

From the ashes of who we once thought we were*

Ash Brockwell

'I hear it in the deep heart's core'

– from 'The Lake Isle of Innisfree' by W. B. Yeats

In the endless spirals of losing and seeking

and finding and losing;

in the making and the breaking and

the kaleidoscope-picture-remaking;

in the names and the labels that we burn, only to be tangled

in other labels and names that we burn; in the tears

that the sunlight shines through to cast dancing rainbows

into the dark corners; and in all of the speaking-places

and the listening-places and the silent places

where there is no more that I can say to you, beloved

of my heart, and you have nothing more to say to me;

in the imagined 'breaking-apart-of-everything'

that turned out to have been

only the breaking-open of a chrysalis;

in the grey misunderstandings that fog the mind;

in all of this, we rise again, like a wisp of woodsmoke
on an autumn evening, only half invisible.

We rise from the tear-soaked ashes
of all we once thought we were,
and leave behind those names that still hurt us,
those embers that still have the power to scorch.

(What if I were to live without a name or a label?
What if I had no title, no pronouns, no papers?
Would I stand in defiance, with one foot
crushing each of the binary boxes,
proclaiming loudly to the world, 'I am Both-at-once-and-neither;
I am All-of-the above-and-more'?
Or would I build myself a small cabin on the lake isle
and live as Yeats and the red squirrels,
on nuts and berries and clear water and Deep Love,
with no heart for announcing that I-am-all-this
or I-am-all-that?)

in the nights when the searing pain of remembering

keeps me from sleep;

in the dark hours before dawn when I walk, skin-soaked,

though a drenched forest;

in the morning sun that cracks the clouds,

and gilds their edges with a glow of hope;

in the mental clamour of unbecoming

all that I was judged to be;

in the endless exchanging

of he-and-him for she-and-her,

in all of this,

I have never quite given up believing in the power of love,

or perhaps I should say Love, with a capital L;

and it is Love that gives me strength to keep breathing.

This is all that I can ask of you.

Only to breathe with me: to trust that the Love

that spins the electrons and the planets

 is as intimately concerned

with the rhythm of our in-breaths and our out-breaths

as with the sparrows that call to us from the garden-hedge,

or the fragments of song that call to us

from ancient soul-worlds forever beyond our reach, or the

wild-spinning colours that our paintbrushes can never tame.

To know that somewhere out beyond all our nonsenses,

all our self-destructive fantasies,

there is still a quiet place

where you and I are as inseparable

as the candle-flame and its glow; and that the falling

of golden leaves, however we might mourn it,

is not the uprooting of the tree.

* From 'TransVerse' exhibition, 2019:
www.ashbrockwell.com/transverse/from-the-ashes

A New Me

Andi Mindel

It was 2008, the digital era well underway.

He broke up with me by text.

I baulk still at the lack of respect.

It was then I stopped to listen to myself,

To allow myself to find myself in myself by myself.

The first years were still and lonely,

Core form consciously unstitched,

and untangled threads left hanging.

Sitting on the outskirts observing the edges,

the in-between, the non-binary,

the neither this nor that.

And this way, I have come to my own peace.

By no means whole, but happier

In the non-conformist interstitial spaces

that defy normative categorisation.

TW: Body changes & dysphoria

(with some euphoria thrown in, because that's how it goes...)

The word 'dysphoria' (derived from a Greek phrase meaning 'difficult to bear') refers to the distress and discomfort that people experience when their personal sense of their gender identity doesn't match the sex they were assigned at birth. Some trans people are conscious of their dysphoria from a very early age, others might have a general feeling of discomfort or 'wrongness' that they don't identify as dysphoria until much later in life, and a few never experience it.

Gender dysphoria can often be treated with a combination of hormones and surgery, although these treatments are unavailable to many people – whether because of cost, waiting times, medical factors or personal reasons – and others might choose not to have them.

The poems in this chapter reflect a variety of different perspectives on dysphoria, starting out light-hearted, and ending up with poems that directly reference its devastating effects.

Specific trigger warnings for individual poems are as follows. Note that 'LH' in brackets indicates that the poem takes a light-hearted look at the subject (otherwise known as a piss-take).

Title	Page	Author	Theme(s)
The Boy	35	Aidan Sarson	Dysphoria in trans men, implied self-harm
Transition Checklist	36	Ash Brockwell	Dysphoria in trans men (LH)
Are You Feeling Better?	38	Frogb0i	Surgery, sex, personal questions (LH)
Ode to Boobies	39	Kay Whitehurst	Breasts, dysphoria in trans women (LH)
Outward, Bound	40	Ash Brockwell	Chest binding, gender euphoria in trans men
Homeward, Unbound	42	Ash Brockwell	Chest binding, dysphoria in trans men
Scars	44	Aidan Sarson	Severe dysphoria, self-harm, chest surgery
Swap Meet	46	Paula Adrianne	General dysphoria (LH)
Shadow	47	Kay Whitehurst	Severe dysphoria, facial hair, depression
Dysphoric Meltdown	48	Ash Brockwell	Gender clinic waiting times, implied suicide

The Boy

Aidan Sarson

Sometimes I look and see,

The boy that hides inside of me,

The boy that never went away,

And eyes the woman with deep dismay.

The boy that couldn't understand,

Why he never became a man,

The boy that wants to maim, destroy,

The woman that stopped the little boy.

And every day, his presence near,

The woman's sanity lives in fear

Will he ever live and thrive,

Killing the woman who kept him alive?

Transition Checklist*

Ash Brockwell

'Chip the glasses and crack the plates / Blunt the knives and bend the forks'
– Dwarf Song from 'The Hobbit', J. R. R. Tolkien

Ditch the make-up and burn the skirts

Change my pronouns and change my name

Tell my friends that my deadname hurts

Wave goodbye to the guilt and shame

Chop my hair off and bind my chest

Lose the perfume and buy cologne

Dress the way that the guys are dressed

Splash my cash on testosterone

Bare my soul on my Facebook page

Say 'Hell, no!' to the 'she' and 'her'

And when I experience `madam rage'

Tell the baristas, 'Please call me sir!'

Dump the heels in a great big bin

Lacy knickers? Yes, chuck them in

(And when I've finished, I'll truly begin

To grieve for the boy I should have been)

And if anyone says I looked better in skirts

Just tell them the truth, that misgendering hurts!

* From 'TransVerse' Exhibition:

www.ashbrockwell.com/transverse/time-for-t

Are you feeling better?

Frogb0i

How are you?

Have you had the surgery?

How long have you been on hormones?

Isn't that a bit hardcore?

Why would you do that? *And are you feeling better?*

Top or bottom?

Do you self-inject?

What do your family think?

Was the recovery painful? *And are you feeling better?*

But you looked SO good before... Why did you choose your name?

Are you still in therapy? And are you feeling better?

Send us a dick pic?

How is it going babes?

Trans boys are "so soft"

How do you have sex?

Do you have a boyfriend? No? Girlfriend?

Are you straight now?

Were you trapped in the wrong body? *And are you feeling better?*

Ode to Boobies

Kay Whitehurst

Boobies, grow, I need you now!
I've fed you hormones, tell me how?
But you just sit there sniggering
Upon my chest, it's sickening.

Jump and bounce like the other girls' do,
Don't just rigidly stick like glue.
My figure needs you, my mental health too,
And your response? – eff you!

If I feed you the right concoction,
Would you be kind and not so obnoxious?
Grow, boobies, grow, you mean more to me
than you'll ever know… please could you be
a little kinder and grow just a bit?
I don't need DD's, just a nice healthy B!

Outward, Bound

Ash Brockwell

'*unbeingdead isn't beingalive*' – *e. e. cummings*

I've been a stranger in this body for forty years
and I never fully knew it?
When you've been used to 'wrong' for sooooooooooooo long,
you have no idea there's a 'right' at all, much less how to do it:
they can tell you over and over that *the body means nothing,*
flesh is only flesh, it's the spirit that matters; it's not about the shape,
the appearance, the look, the style. But what they don't tell you,
meanwhile, is this: there's a physicality to the soul, a bliss
in embodiment when lies shatter and your own truth
is made whole; a sublime joy when the shape you see in the mirror
finally matches the template laid down inside.
Bound flat, I feel like *me*, for the first time.

Do you take it for granted when you're cis?
Is it only when the truth has been denied with every nerve,
or, at best, reduced to a fantasy that you know you don't deserve,
or the shameful secret that you've always got to hide: is it only then
that you find such pure delight in letting yourself be real?
Or is this, in fact, the way that *most* people feel?

Are we the only ones who had to detach to survive,

who had to deny every feeling, stifle every emotion,

lock down all sensation and focus on unbeingdead,

because we never knew there was an option of beingalive instead?

Euphoria reverberates through my chest; with each breath

I bind my wandering soul back into this flesh,

and finally start to arrive

in this body that was never truly mine before.

The train speeds onward. Facing outward, finding my voice:

This is me. Believe, or don't believe: your choice. Your disbelief

says more about you. Hand on the heart that beats in this flat chest,

I know it's true. That's all I'll say.

Outward.

Onward.

This heart knows the way. Held tight within

this second skin, supported, safe, secure, I breathe

the rightness in; ask myself yet again…

where have I been for so long, and how (in the name of all

that's beautiful) did I never understand

what it was that felt so wrong?

* From 'TransVerse' exhibition:
www.ashbrockwell.com/transverse/outward-bound

Homeward, Unbound

Ash Brockwell

Euphoria is a wonderful thing.

You know the plan. You have eight hours, anyhow,

to be yourself. It'll all be fine. The clock…starts… NOW!

The countdown has begun: minutes left, four hundred and sixty-nine.

Well, what on earth are you waiting for, man?

Don't waste another one!

Eight hours to be myself? You insane, or having a laugh?

That's seven gone.

Get lost.

Seven and three-quarters. Eight.

Forget it.

Eight and a half.

Oh, come on, mate, not yet.

Nine. Ten.

Ah, just a BIT longer?

Eleven and three-quarters. Then

it's back to this, as it always is.

Back to the inner battle, once again.

It's unwinnable, either way. Should I give in to fear?

Am I already too weak to persevere, not brave enough

to hold my nerve, an undeserving coward

curling my broken identity inwards and down

as a dark smog of dysphoria suffocates my soul?

Or am I now too stubborn to let go,

squeezing ribs, restricting breath,

until the aching in my lungs and sides

consumes all other thoughts and denies me peace?

In the end, I know release *must* come: I must let go,

or fracture into pieces in a silent crack of pain.

I close the doors behind me after I unbind,

and.. breathe…

and what is left of me lets out a sigh:

a deep sigh of relief mingled with despair.

I am only half the man I was before.

I have lost my rhythm, lost all interest in rhyme.

I have lost the spark of self-assurance that made me feel, briefly,

that I could own this body;

lost the war that I was fighting against myself.

Soul or body, one must always lose:

there are no winners in this game.

Scars

Aidan Sarson

The scars on my chest still visible

They replaced the ones I made myself,

Decorated my left arm with slices

With a razor

Or a scalpel

Not too deep, was never that brave

But deep enough

The sound, the tear of skin

Then wait.........

The red, the tiny buds of blood

Random pattern along the incision

All growing, getting bigger, merging, flowing

The warm line of blood finding its way to the ground,

leaving a sticky tangy trail

I can smell the blood even now, can taste the metal tang

Just one cut though....

Not enough

Again, slice again

This time slice three times quickly,

Then stop and watch the show again

Hurt the body that causes so much pain.

I can barely see those scars now

replaced by the two on my chest.

Swap Meet

Paula Adrianne

When I don't like my shift
I swap it with a mate
She does my early
And I do her late.

When I have a full English
I'm not keen on fried bread
So I ask the cafe owner
For a piece of toast instead.

But it's not the same with body parts
You can't just do a swap,
So we have to take hormones
And face a scary op.

It'd be amazing if we could swap
Trans women and trans men
We'd organise a swap meet
From eight until half ten.

But that isn't yet possible
So transitioning's what I do
The journey's long and hard
But I will see it through!

Shadow

Kay Whitehurst

Journal, Journal, burning bright,

What lingering words should I write?

My pain, the hurt I see in the mirror?

The disgust? Or should I be more polite?

Rhymes of fairies and rainbows and peace?

Because most of those don't happen for me!

Locked in this infernal hell

called a soul, begging for my release.

I look, I stare, I stand, I bare all

to the silence of my heart, who knows not how

to best take this share before I fall

violently into this loathing pit of self-hatred.

I dread it all.

To look up and see the shadow of a beard,

Instead of the sleek figure of a woman standing tall.

Dysphoric Meltdown (Running Out Of Time)

Ash Brockwell

With respect, Health Secretary, we are running out of time.

I refer, of course, to my patients who have been

In a state of dysphoric meltdown

since I first referred them to a gender clinic

in the year two thousand and sixteen.

The average waiting time in some clinics

has now exceeded three and a half years:

that's a total of 42 months, 182 weeks,

or approximately 1,274 days.

Have you the slightest idea what that might feel like?

Do you even have a clue what I'm talking about?

I doubt it. Dysphoria probably isn't something

that you think about a lot. Don't be offended,

but perhaps an example will bring it home to you.

Imagine waking up one day and finding –

certain parts of your anatomy had gone missing,

replaced by something that wasn't meant to be there.

Don't try to tell me you wouldn't care. Even pissing

wouldn't happen the way it was intended.

Now imagine you had to wait 1300 days to speak

to someone who would make you an appointment to speak

to someone else after another nine months to a year,

and at that second appointment

they'd make a third, at which (after yet another year)

you'd talk to them to them both and they'd interview your wife,

(which is absurd, you have to admit, but hey, that's life).

And even after all that, they'd still say, 'Wait a bit...'

So you'd try to complain

but it would all be in vain and you'd write a letter

to the Health Secretary –

oh, sorry, you *are* the Health Secretary – I mean the Prime

Minister, and say, 'With respect, Prime Minister,

this is shit, and I am running out of time, and it isn't

a matter for debating; the simple fact is that no human being

can possibly endure this much waiting,'

And the Prime Minister would simply shrug and say,

'That's life, I'm afraid, but don't worry,

it will all be so much better after Brexit.

I simply don't understand why you're in such a hurry to fix it.'

And you'd give him a despairing look

and say, `All I want is to be me,

to be complete, the way that I was meant to be.

Is that really such a crime?'

With respect, Health Secretary,

this is the unendurable situation

of the patients that I referred to the gender clinic in 2016.

Perhaps you'll have a little more empathy,

now you understand exactly what I mean?

There are certain things that one can do,

of course, behind the scenes,

which provide temporary relief for a couple of years.

But one dares not speak of those.

(One is likely to get some grief if one interferes

with the cash cows that are shamelessly milked

by members of the Establishment, I suppose.)

I am not saying for a moment that I condone

such practices. But I have to concur

that my patient would not have been alive today,

without a brave ex-colleague who must remain nameless;

and in private, I am grateful to her.

With all due respect, Health Secretary,

you are not blameless in this mess.

If patients with cancer were being told to wait

a minimum of five years just to get a date

for their life-saving surgery to be carried out,

and by that time it was tragically too late,

you'd certainly have to answer to the press.

'Ah well,' you say. 'You can't possibly compare the two.

Dysphoria doesn't kill.'

But I tell you, we are running out of time;

and if you don't do something soon,

it will.

* From 'TransVerse' Exhibition, 2019:

www.ashbrockwell.com/transverse/meltdown

TW: Facing transphobia

Trans people often complain that the word 'transphobia' is inaccurate. As someone put it in a recent Facebook debate: 'They're not *scared* of us, they're just assholes!' Nonetheless, it's still more widely used and understood than the alternative, 'transmisia', which refers specifically to hatred or aggression directed against trans people.

Whichever word you use to describe it, the likelihood is that most trans people have experienced it many times. If dysphoria feels like fighting a losing battle with your own body, facing transphobia (or transmisia) can feel like fighting a losing battle with society.

The poems in this chapter, some lighter and others deadly serious, describe our experiences of being hated, mocked, rejected by family members, verbally abused or even violently attacked – just for being who we are. As such, even the 'lighter' ones don't always make easy reading for trans people: if you're feeling mentally fragile today, this chapter and the next one might be best avoided. If, on the other hand, you're looking for something to spit back (metaphorically) in the faces of online trolls or hostile media, you'll find plenty of inspiration!

Trigger warnings for the poems in this chapter are as follows (LH = light-hearted):

Title	Page	Author	Theme(s)
Apache Attack Helicopter	54	Kay Whitehurst	Transphobia (LH)
People say	57	Aidan Sarson	Transphobia and homophobia (LH)
Transactivist	58	Ash Brockwell	Media transphobia (LH)
Trans Etiquette...	60	Ash Brockwell	Transphobia (LH)
The Raze of Ecology	65	Megan Nightingale	Ecocide, transphobia
Dear 'mum'	66	Alex Bear	Rejection, transphobic families
Double Figures	68	Ash Brockwell	Fear of rejection, dysphoria
Gender Babylon	70	The Bleeding Obvious	General transphobia, transmisogyny
Cis lies	74	Frogb0i	Transphobia, racism
Stigma	75	Megan Nightingale	General transphobia
Born to Drown	76	Kay Whitehurst	Transphobia, depression
Sometimes Waving...	78	Ash Brockwell	Transphobia, violence, depression
Flames of Hate	82	Vanilla (RTI)	Transphobic violence
Refugee	84	Julie (RTI)	Transphobic violence

Apache Attack Helicopter – a song

Kay Whitehurst

The growing disease among the popular masses

Walking around and kissing managers' asses

Feeling each other in inappropriate ways

Denying climate change and every natural disaster

The present level of overwhelming reaction

To people on the outside of their little faction

Is to kick us down and give us verbal abuse

But now what are we doing? We're gonna....

Identify as an Apache Attack Helicopter

Identify as a marshmallow and suck in the laughter

Take away their insults and turn them to pride

Identify as anything that you feel inside

Binary trans and NB friends all together

We can identify as the guy on the weather

Or rip our shirts in two, identify as the hulk

Kick it to the masses show we don't give a fuck about YOU.

Drowning in the pool of stagnant stand-up retorts
Dissing us like they've some sort of knowledge or cause
To be a one with our circle, or to join in our pride
Then joke about us like they've got an insider's right.

But jokes belong to us, we're gonna wear 'em and laugh
Those other comic fuckers can go land on their ass
We don't give a shit about the state of your act
We're not gonna react, we're just gonna.....

Identify as an Apache Attack Helicopter
Identify as a marshmallow and suck in the laughter
Take away their insults and turn them to pride
Identify as anything that you feel inside
Binary trans and NB friends all together
We can identify as the guy on the weather
Or rip our shirts in two, identify as the hulk
Kick it to the masses show we don't give a fuck about YOU.

Corvette Chevy,
A Pint of Heavy,
The Queen Elizabeth carrier in the Royal Navy

A Llama,

No Drama,

A petting zoo in downtown Atlanta

We identify however the fuck we want

The onus is on you to put up your decent front

And practice as you preach about leaving alone

Anyone who doesn't damage either you or your own.

And God forbid you should ever find

You wake up different, maybe deaf or blind?

Then you'll find out what it's like to be

The butt of the joke. You get me?

People say…

Aidan Sarson

People say, because I'm gay,
I ought to act a certain way,
A little camp, a little fey.

People say, because I'm trans,
Were you born a woman, or a man?
They can't work out where I began.

People say, because I'm trans and gay,
Well, surely that's straight, not gay?
And try to wipe my existence away.

Transactivist

Ash Brockwell

I thought that I was innocent, I don't quite understand,
The *Times* has bought my story and It's all got out of hand.
I'm now the public enemy, it doesn't make much sense:
I'm fairly sure my only crime Is peeing in the Gents.

But now they're blaming me, they say, for this destructive fashion
Of listening to children and of showing them compassion,
For sex and gender are the same, as bigots all agree:
If anyone thinks differently, they're catching it from me!

It's all my fault when little girls refuse to play princesses,
And boys throw out their footballs and insist on wearing dresses.
'It won't end there,' they darkly mutter, while inventing dramas
Of schools where half the pupils now identify as llamas.

They claim I've barged in spaces where I clearly don't belong,
Denied the truth of science and just can't admit I'm wrong:
A pervert and a criminal, I thrive on starting fights,
I've trespassed in the swimming pool and torn up women 's rights.

They've let me have my way, they say, for far too long already:

I've undermined society until it's quite unsteady,

Contaminated toilets with my trans-infested breath,

And dealt the Patriarchy blows that may yet cause its death.

They say they know the truth at last: they've found out my agenda

Of causing floods and killing God and redefining gender.,

And - here's the worst - annihilating nature as we know it!

There's nothing more that I can do...except become a poet.

* From 'TransVerse' Exhibition, 2019:

www.ashbrockwell.com/transverse/hidden-agenda

Trans Etiquette for Beginners

Ash Brockwell

Basic Principles

When you discover someone's trans,
don't tell them that it isn't true.
Don't ask them why they've made this 'choice',
or why they're 'doing this to you'.

Don't tell them it's the 'latest trend',
or ask how long this 'phase' will last;
Don't say you loved them as they were,
and sob at photos from the past.

Don't ask them what their old name was –
or if you know, don't call them by it.
Don't EVER ask them what they've got
between their legs. Just don't dare try it.

Medical Intervention, or the lack of it

Don't ask them if they've had 'The Op',
or when they plan on having it.
(For those on three-year waiting lists,
such questions make them feel like shit,
And some folks can't have surgery,
and others just don't want an op;
So, even if you're curious, i
t's not your business. Please, just stop.)

Don't ask them when their boobs will grow,
or when they think they'll get a beard;
If people asked YOU stuff like that,
you'd roll your eyes and call them weird.

Pronouns

Don't say, 'To me, you're always SHE;
I'll never think of you as HE.'
Don't say, 'To me, you're always HE;
I'll never think of you as SHE.'

And if they're neither SHE nor HE,

for pity's sake, don't ever say,

'The pronoun THEY is plural, and

there's one of you; you can't be THEY!'

You may hear other pronouns too,

and if a person says they're XE,

Or ZEM or VE or EY or FAE...

well, who are you to disagree?

You ask why we're obsessed with pronouns:

tell me, then, if you're a dude,

And someone called you SHE and HER,

you wouldn't find them rather rude?

Or if you're female – Mrs, Miss or Ms –

just think, if someone called you 'sir',

You wouldn't feel at all upset?

You wouldn't change their HIM to HER?

If everyone misgendered you,

you'd rage and shout and make a fuss.

It sucks. It hurts. It just feels wrong.

So please don't do the same to us.

Media

The media is full of crap:

"My kid caught trans, and yours might too!

They'll get it from a YouTube star,

 and maybe pass it on to you!

They're all erasing lesbians!

Why can't they just accept they're gay?

I used to be transgender, now

I'm saved: I'll teach you how to pray!

Trans women in the ladies' loo?

They'll rape your daughters while they pee!"

Ignore the lot of them, my friend.

You know the truth, and so do we.

A Side Note on Public Toilets

It isn't rocket science, so

I won't spend too much time on this.

Trans women in the ladies' loo?

Just leave them be and let them piss.

A Bit of Positivity

By now you might be thinking,
'Is there nothing I'm allowed to say?
Trans people are too difficult:
I think I'd better stay away!'

But just before you make that choice,
please stop and ponder for a minute,
And ask yourself, 'What would my life
be like, without these people in it?'

Don't whine about free speech, and say
you're not 'politically correct':
It's really not that difficult
to treat your friends with due respect.

The Raze of Ecology

Megan Nightingale

Austere in sunlight, canvassing acres of terrain,

existed a desolate plain.

Strewn with the felling of a thousand and one lives.

Each torn, ripped and sliced from life.

A magnificent oak transformed into a bruised stump.

In tandem to the trees lay foliage debris,

biodiversity executed for capitalistic means,

organisms made homeless, withering in the sun,

shrouded in pandemonium.

Exposed to further savagery; torn from fellow vegetation. Alone.

Declining in a desolate patchwork of JCB; monoculture;

biological anguish.

From this, modern metropolis was born.

Built from systematic felling, the creation of concrete and

its grey architecture; dull and seeping,

its homogenous pallor felling species.

Policy trees slow the spreading grey veneer, but for how long?

Section 28 was eradicated, but has it left all untainted?

Dear `mum'

Alex Bear

Dear `mum',

I knew from the way you clipped your vowels down the phone

that you would never meet your son.

It was with that voice usually reserved for cold-callers

that you said goodbye.

I didn't choose to be trans;

I only chose not to die.

Your son has a beard now, dad

He lives loudly and proudly, through good and bad,

Perhaps someday I'll tell you how.

Or perhaps not;

because I love myself too much to bother trying now.

Your big bro's voice has changed now, sister,

It's deep and rich and sounds so much more like me,

Though some days it's barely a whisper,

Like the secrets we once shared back home.

I waited months, praying one of you would call,

when the call never came I chose to love myself twice as hard;

enough for myself and those lost, all.

Do you even miss my birthday cards?

But I'll not think on your absence too long

For choosing life is never wrong.

I'll walk my path with joy and pride

and marvel at the man I've discovered inside.

I'll celebrate my journey without you

Because that's what those in exile do.

We love a little harder,

We hold each other a little longer.

We know the value of `just' one more hug,

Or rooibos made in our favourite mug

But we know how much self-love costs:

Sometimes the price of living is to become one of the `lost'.

Double Figures

Ash Brockwell

I wish I could have loved that paisley dress
you gave me on the day that I turned ten.
(If I were male, would you love me less?)

I smiled through my tears, my mind a mess.
'You're double figures now,' you told me then.
I wish I could have loved that paisley dress.

I had no words, no language to express
my grief for years that wouldn't come again.
(You didn't want a boy. You'd love me less.)

Grow up, move on, conceal, deny, repress,
Yet still the image lingers, now and then:
I wish I could have loved that paisley dress.

It's only now, at forty, I confess
my deepest dream: to join the world of men,
And live as Me. (But will you love me less?)

Perhaps this truth will shatter my success;

But if not Me, then who? If not now, when?

I never could have loved that paisley dress.

(I wonder if you love me any less?)

* From 'TransVerse' exhibition, 2019:
www.ashbrockwell.com/transverse/double-figures

Gender Babylon (a song)

The Bleeding Obvious

Last night, she wore the dress

Put those closet fears to the test

Stepping outside with the wind on her face

Up at three in a club someplace.

Dance the night away

Dance the pain away

Chameleon by day, herself by night

Then at the end when the shutters come down

Back to the daytime job in town.

The guys all point and jeer

Because of the fear inside her.

And the implication is

Because she's in between she's neither.

It's not a phase

It's not a craze

New attitudes and platitudes

Keep hanging on

Be set upon

Your friends are gone for gender babylon.

Days at home, hiding the clothes

Change in a layby hidden by shadows

The other day she came out to a friend

Someone else who thinks it's a trend.

Hoping for the courage to go see a man

Who can maybe help her form a plan.

But the strength is elusive, the days are draining

Painfully aware that time is passing.

The girls all point and sneer

Because of the fear inside her.

And the implication is

Now she's crossed the line she's neither.

It's not a phase

It's not a craze

New attitudes and platitudes

Keep hanging on

Be set upon

Your friends are gone for gender babylon.

She won and lost and she won again.

The question wasn't if but a definite when.

Jennifer, Emily, Zoe or Lisa

Pick a name and hope it suits ya.

Losing friends, unwanted attention

Losing family and marital tension

Never can stop coming out

History snapping at her heels throughout.

The children stop and stare

Because of the fear inside her.

And the implication is

Because she's in between she's neither.

It's not a phase

It's not a craze

New attitudes and platitudes

Keep hanging on

Be set upon

Your friends are gone for gender babylon.

Him. Her. Mrs. She. Ms. Mister. They. It.

Me. You. Pink. Blue. Girl. Boy. Them. It.

And the days are long but the nights are longer

And the days are long, but I'm getting stronger.

From the album 'Rainbow Heart':
http://bleedingobvious.uk/rainbowheart

Cis Lies

Frogb0i

Fi Fi Fo Thumb

I smell the blood of a cis white man

Rebuild a new world in the ruins of the old

"All cops are bastards" never gets old.

Check your privilege before you open your mouth,

Open your eyes before you open your mouth,

She holds her bag close as the black youth walk by,

She puts her keys in her knuckles, won't look me in the eye.

Burn masculinity into the ground

Existing is hard enough without all these cis lies

Stigma

Megan Nightingale

Stigma,

what should be an enigma to all,

can be the minority's downfall,

if allowed to stand tall.

Unconscious or otherwise,

full of reprise for,

all that defy societal drives for,

arid bleached skin; popular sexuality.

Built from malice and scorn,

fearful of diversity and all that protrudes as,

love for being, not anatomy.

Difference, not similarity.

Stigma,

the enemy of acceptance, characterised by rejection.

Born to Drown

Kay Whitehurst

Born to drown

A 2-fold frown both

Inside and out

Carries the clout of the world

whose tears

spread down the years

and pool in the moment where

life departs, we face our fears.

The world rumbles by.

Incessant nagging, society tagging

our bodies sagging.

Hate festers on, its immediate son

Violence begun, and barrage the weak

With tales, tittle tattle

Unthinkable prattle from the mouth of a twit

Makes you feel like shit.

This world doesn't care

The beauty you bare

rots like a corpse in the cool midnight air.

No thought your own

to the values you're thrown, straight after birth.

Make your own way or die trying

Dream of you flying

but crash in a world full of razors and lying

there on your own, all alone

you can't fight with life, it wins every time.

Sometimes Waving but Mostly Drowning*

Ash Brockwell

"I was much too far out all my life / And not waving but drowning" – Stevie Smith

Page after page, the shit rolls in:

hysterical headlines that seem so real

to those beyond our circle, inked in lies,

telling the middle-class bigots

that we're the target group they're still permitted to despise.

Page after page.

Wave after wave of mindless rage.

As if our eyes can't see, our hearts can't feel.

Thugs on the streets or the buses,

throwing rocks or punches at us for holding hands.

Mumsnet mums on their phones throwing digital slurs,

as they pack their children's lunches

in eco-friendly paper bags and tie

pink bands around their perfect plaits:

all of them running so scared

because we, the gender rebels, dared

to cut our hair and wear

a shirt and tie, and live as the men we are;

or grow our hair and wear

a skirt and tights, and live as the women that we are;

or dye our hair multiple shades of blue and wear

rainbow unicorn socks

and refuse to tick ANY fucking gender box

(or indeed any combination of the above that might suggest

for a millisecond that we love and accept ourselves the way

we truly are)… none of it matters, in the end,

because the only way to play

the game is their way, they say: to shine the masks up, and pretend.

Conform, they tell us; heaven knows we tried, we *tried,*

we thought we could forget

the truth of who we always were, and just play small, and hide…

until the weight of masks began to suffocate us,

and the exhaustion of pretence began to break us

somewhere deep inside…until the moment came to realise

it was *this or die…*

and some chose this, and others died.

Our non-compliance is a threat, or so it seems,

to the existence of their dreams

of Man-the-Head; to the extent

that in the eyes, still blurred with lies,

of those who think they know it all,

we would be better dead.

Our flag is life and hope, within our circle; but to them

offensive, painting the sky with

words they wish they never had to hear.

And still, wave after wave, the shit rolls nearer.

Photographs of those they hurt. Nazis escorted by police,

to keep them safe while they attack our Pride.

(And what about OUR safety? Don't we count?)

Swastikas flying freely, flouting law,

and our flag trampled in the dirt and blood and mud...

and we, thrown here and there by every wave,

half-broken, all exhausted, wash up now in some dark cave,

as with our final strength we gather up the remnants of our flag

from seaweed-slimy rocks,

and wash the stink of fascists from our skin;

and yet again,

the mothers, frowning as we proclaim our right to breathe,

begin a new petition.

And we are here,

still here,

still calling out for allies

to join our coalition of the brave,

sometimes waving...

but, if I'm honest,

mostly drowning.

* From 'TransVerse' exhibition, 2019:
www.ashbrockwell.com/transverse/mostly-drowning

Flames of Hate

Vanilla (Refugee Trans Initiative)

Three transgender women

attacked by neighbours

who say, and I quote,

"we will make sure you return to your sinful country

and stop you from exposing your stupidity

however way we can...

even if we have to kill you."

These were the words

of an angry neighbourhood.

Forced into eviction,

stuck in Nairobi

with no place to call home,

they are traumatized by

this all unfortunate incident.

The flames of hate are still blazing

and it's us, the transgender refugees,

in the centre of this furnace...

Kicked out of rental homes on a daily basis.

No protection. Nowhere to go.

And the fear of arrest and forcefully allocating

some of our brothers and sisters

to a hostile environment

where they face hurt and death.

Those in the urban areas are no difference

to this cruel hostile country we are in,

after fleeing our homes from the same persecution

family and the community at large was showing us…

The police are hunting us down

and treating us like trash every day

just because of our status:

we have nowhere to run to,

we are not safe!

LGBTI refugees in Kenya need intervention,

especially we the trans, who are being erased

on a daily basis.

We call upon everyone supporting our community

to hear our cries,

for many of us have shed enough blood

and are still facing trauma in this unaccepting country.

We have to stand with each other

so as to protect the lives of our sisters

in such an unfortunate situation.

Refugee

Julie (Refugee Trans Initiative)

being trans woman,

more so a refugee,

is the most painful and cruel status

anyone should have!

through the abuses and trauma

trans women,

more so refugees,

have no voices and are

almost invisible

to the LGBI community!

84

TW: Remembering our dead

November 20th, Trans Day of Remembrance, was started in 1998 by Rita Hester in protest that the murders of her trans friends were being ignored by the lesbian, gay and bisexual community and the wider media. It's a day to remember and mourn all our trans and non-binary siblings around the world who lost their lives to violence, suicide or medical neglect in the past twelve months.

Yet it's also a day to rise up together against the ongoing loss of life, especially among trans women of colour, whose life expectancy in the USA has been calculated by university researchers as 35 – in comparison to 81 for white cisgender women. Many are misgendered and deadnamed by the media even after their death. Because of the intersection of racism, misogyny and transphobia, trans women of colour continue to face appalling discrimination and exclusion in housing, education, and employment, as well as unjustified police harassment. That's why TDOR-related blogs and memes often include the phrase 'mourn the dead and fight like hell for the living'.

The poems in this chapter all have trigger warnings for death, most also for violence, one ('Little Star') for bereavement by stillbirth, and one ('Driven to kill') for suicide.

The first three - Kay Whitehurst's *Trans Day of Remembrance*, Ash Brockwell's *A Messy Remembrance*, and Tina Cross's *Transgender Poem of Remembrance* - were written specifically for TDOR. Some of the poems and song lyrics in the last chapter of this book might also find a place in TDOR events, reminding us to hold on to hope and keep living our best lives in memory of those we've lost.

Trans Day of Remembrance

Kay Whitehurst

Falling into the depths of negativity once more,

The dreaded bleakness of a mind overcome with grief.

The time, it seems, was taken much too quickly,

By some great faceless nameless thief.

Their path was short, their footsteps buried,

Some may not have known their struggle.

Beyond what they saw on the great façade,

Happiness dispensed by a clinical drug.

But people they were and people they remain,

in our memories and in our hearts,

The Almighty keeps them close for ever,

Their love flows from the ramparts.

They were our brothers, lovers, sisters, friends,

Mothers, fathers, the list never ends.

The strength of our spirit shall never weary

Our thoughts and prayers, them they defend.

The seas may roll in and out, the light may fade,

The snow may fall and be melted again by the spring.

Without them here it seems pointless and dull,

And hardly worth the time for living.

But remember that they are with us still,

They never shall leave us again.

Their smiles and laughs live on forever.

We Will Remember Them.

A Messy Remembrance*

Ash Brockwell

This is what the trans flag

really looks like.

It isn't pretty.

It isn't perfect pastel stripes

of pink and white and baby blue.

It's the fragments of yourself

that you keep digging out

with bleeding fingers

from the mud of everyone's expectations

of who you would-could-should have been.

It's the bits that you cling to

when you're too tired to go on

but you go on anyway, because of a Someone,

or several someones, or a Somewhere,

or even a Somewhen;

or because of a song you haven't sung yet, or

a crazy dream that nobody else understands,

or the colours of next autumn, or the scent

of the cinnamon rolls you haven't baked yet,

or just because of all those who didn't.

(This was supposed to be a simple painting

for Trans Day of Remembrance.

Neat lines of text making up a neat candle.

In blue: WE.

In pink: WILL.

In white: REMEMBER.

In pink: THEM.

In blue: #TDOR.

But anyone who knows me at all

knows I am not someone

who can do neat.

Or simple.

But grief is a messy thing

anyway. It doesn't stay compliantly

into boxes; it can't be encased in files

or folders. It has an unpleasant habit

of surfacing at unexpected times.

So maybe, after all,

a messy remembrance

is enough?)

* From 'TransVerse' exhibition, 2019:
www.ashbrockwell.com/transverse/messy-remembrance

Transgender Poem of Remembrance

Tina Cross

Midnight rain, or Transgender tears,

So many lost throughout the years.

Murder, suicide, it's all the same.

Beaten, taunted, driven insane.

A coldness still pervades the land,

Like icy fingers on ungloved hand.

For all that never reached their goals

Let them live on within our souls.

For each one lost, a candle burns

A glimmer of hope as this world turns

Let all of those that see the light

Let us live on, as is our right

Let their deaths not be in vain.

They help to stop the midnight rain.

Little Star

Kim

Twinkle twinkle, Little Star

I can see you, there you are

Sitting there upon a cloud

How you make your parents proud

See you soon, Little Star

We know that you have not gone far

When we see your star at night

We know it's you, you're shining bright

Love you always, Little Star

We hope you're happy where you are

We've seen your star up in the sky

And now we've come to say Goodbye

Why This Girl Cries

Paula Adrianne

The parents who ignore her

Believing it's a trend

The child who abandoned her

That used to be a friend

The sniggers as she walks past

The whispers that she hears

Just one or two reasons

Her eyes are full of tears

The cousin she can't visit

Banished by her aunt

Too scared to use school toilets

She almost wets her pants

They way her body is changing

In a way that she hates

The gauntlet she has to run

Outside the school gates.

Deliberate misgendering

In order to be mean

The smirk of her teacher

Who fails to intervene

The constant dead naming

Hurts like a broken bone

That's why she's in her room

That's why she cries alone.

Why This Girl Dies (the same girl - 15 years later)

Paula Adrianne

Failing to pass

Due to a hirsute face

Right wing hate groups

Such as 'A Women's Place'

Transphobic TV shows

Loose Women et al

Germaine fucking Greer

And all of her rotten pals

Trump's transphobia

A world full of hate

A vulnerable trans girl

Who has to work late

TERFs on Facebook

Society's biggest blight

Lack of policing

Rise of the right

She's erased by the media

In their transphobic trends

She's dropped by her family

She's dropped by her friends

No guards on the late night train

There's no one on her side

That is why we lost her

That's why this girl died

When we die, we lose 21 Grams,

they say this is how much a soul weighs.

RKP

Orion's belt has passed 180 degrees,

Around a house that is not mine.

I am belonging now to doorsteps,

Asking to sleep with snakes,

With welcoming host nests on sofas.

Smoke is blown –

Protective rings form above our heads.

Friendship can be found in strangers' faces.

My stomach is a knot of homesickness –

Worse when there is no "Home."

You're only a stone's throw away,

Yet further than before.

The spit from those words still hang in the air,

Like blunt cuts throbbing they vibrate,

Describing a person…

Un-wantable

Un-lovable.

Un-suitable.

My colours are an antibiotic grey,

They bleed in to the rain,

Faded from a purple bruising chest.

Eyes wide like mirrored mirages on the edge of the universe,

Asking that age old question,

"Why is this happening?"

Heidi says, "It's abuse."

N'the ground hits my head cos the carpet was ripped…

Her gravity of standard has bent kind light false, no patience,

Like dead stars & black holes.

Kneeled down in precious stone pressure,

Panic attacks & circumstance reassure,

That my 21 grams are not enough.

Re-vocalised verbs devalue my validity –

They are reminisced to remain,

Cos Anger meant it this time.

The only thing I did

Kay Whitehurst

One in the arm and one in the thigh

One in the temple and one in the eye

Rivers run quick, deep and red to the source

Watching the anger of the murderer's curse

Why should I? I sob and cry

Why should I be the one to die?

I paid my bills on time every time

yet here I am, on the floor I lie

They laugh and they sneer as they

put in the boot,

Make sure I'm gone and take all the loot.

The only crime I'm guilty of, was

looking quite cute.

But when they found out my masculine past

Their rage spilled right over, why did they ask?

Cos the only thing I did to die at their hands

Was to walk in the street when I'm openly trans.

Driven to kill

Kim

This story I'll tell you

Will make you feel sad

It'll make you feel angry

It'll make you feel mad

For this is a story

About trouble and pain

That ends with a loss

There was nothing to gain!

It started that day

When they followed me home

They pushed and they kicked

Wouldn't leave me alone

Then each day that followed

It became worse and worse

I don't know why they did it

Perhaps I was cursed?

So one night all alone

I took to my room

and I thought to myself

"it'll be over soon"

With no fear in my heart

and naught but a knife

I slashed my own wrists

I took my own life

As the blood dripped away

and my heart stood still

Those kids were to blame

They drove me to kill

They're lucky, you see

cos now they got away

and my family lives

with this pain every day

Cos I am not there

they all weep and they cry

for no one could save me

They all watched me die

So when you see a kid

who's not pretty or smart

Don't taunt them or beat them

Please, have a heart

'Cos one day that kid

That you kicked in the head

may be found by her parents too

in her room,

dead.

We are more than just a gender!

(And now for a bit of light relief after all that talk of death…)

The poems in this chapter are a mixed bag. They touch on a very wide range of themes, including love, spiritual transformation, heterochromia (the phenomenon of having different coloured eyes), tiredness, hair, reminiscences, train travel, stepping outside your comfort zone, coding, social media, road rage, nature meditation, and many more. But one thing you *won't* find in this chapter is any mention of transitioning, or indeed anything to do with gender identity at all - because, guess what, #TransPeopleArePeople and #WeHaveLivesToo.

For most people, this chapter should be relatively free of potentially triggering topics (although, as before, we can't make any guarantees).

Summertime romance

Kay Whitehurst

Summertime breathes an air of romance

a world seldom seen, caught swinging in a flashdance

of passion and heat and hearts sewn as one

where the two souls meet, to become only one

where the ties of the worldly bonds are undone

lying there in your arms

my feelings alive

with you every second rivals all that have gone

and rests in your deep ink-well eyes.

Trousseau

Jani E Z Franck

I dreamt I collected all the pieces

of my heart

that I had given away.

The first was in your back pocket,

flat and forgotten.

The next was wrapped around

with a lock of my hair,

faded and crumbling.

You'd let the next piece roll under our bed,

it lay there gathering dust.

The next piece had been burnished gold

by your voice,

a soft sliver of shining metal in your outstretched hand,

you returned it with a smile

and said you had never forgotten me.

It was hidden in secret
where you'd not once thought to look.

It was in a box of blue feathers
waiting for the right moment.

It was hidden in secret
where you guarded it still
and lifted it out of the dark
each full moon.

On a wall with other hearts.

At the bottom of a stream,
rolled soft edges amongst the pebbles.

In a cave with the firelight flickering
on the walls, making its shadow huge
and ominous.

It was falling, falling into the endless
darkness you chose.
It lay at the bottom of your staircase
like a shard from a glass slipper.

It bled silently to death
on the hard ground.

It was backstage still waiting for a cue.

It was there on the beach
where we first kissed.

It was in your mother's kitchen.

It nestled on your breast
with your hands resting lightly over it.

It lay covered in stitched together leaves.

It was in the drawer
where you hid your gold coins.

It was wrapped in tissue paper
and scented with lavender in an old wardrobe.

It was in your garden, of course,
well watered and blossoming.

With the love I gave out,
I stitch these pieces together
and fold them inside my chest.

Wrap them in rose petals.
Return them to flame and water.

With the love I got back,
I heal the places
where the pieces don't quite fit.

This is my heart,
this is my heart
and I claim it for my own
and for no other.

Distracted

Kestral Gaian

Momentarily. Involuntarily.

We see someone. Chemicals.
We feel something. Desire.
We want something. Closeness.

Feelings stir. Limbs stir.
Your heart beats faster.

In less than a second your body has
taken control
of your mind.

Taken control
of your senses.

Taken control
of your world.

Fight or flight.

Hot or hotter.

Subconscious lust.

Conscious shame.

And a second later...

Life goes on.

The Alchemist's Dream - a song*

Ash Brockwell

Break us again, O Beloved!

For whenever you break us,

You gather us up with such infinite tenderness

That in some distant whisper or some distant vision,

Our souls learn your innermost song in the silence,

And your hands will remake us

With a Love that we cannot express…

Yes, there are those who survive this lifetime intact,

Yes, there are those who hold firm and refuse to surrender…

But where is the magic and where is the rapture in that?

For we only become our true selves in the hands of the Mender.

Break us again, O Beloved!

For whenever you break us,

The heat of your flame sparks a melody in our veins,

And the songs that we sing start to echo your mystery,

Till some of the listeners find their own echoes…

And the places they take us

Are the places where power remains.

Break us again, O Beloved!

For whenever you break us,

And mend us with gold, there's a trace of your Love revealed;

Transformation is wrought by the cruellest of breaking,

And the deepest surrender, and the sweetest remaking...

Till they start to mistake us

For the Alchemist's vision fulfilled...

Nothing remains of the people we were,

Nothing remains of the life we once knew;

Though our substance is clay, yet we shimmer with gold,

And we look at each other, and see only You...

So at last, in this lifetime, the Alchemist's dream is fulfilled!

* From 'TransVerse' exhibition, 2019:
www.ashbrockwell.com/transverse/rough-kintsugi

Storm

Devin Valentine

I can hear you coming in over the water

All I know is I'm supposed to be here in this moment

Inside the storm

It's not violent

It's peaceful

More peaceful than humanity

We project our failure onto nature, but

We are not a storm

We are just us

We could never be the storm

The storm will be here long after we are gone

And we will be gone

In this moment I am alive

But I think about being alone

I wish I wasn't alone

I try to relish my experience

Being present, but I am presently alone

Try not to worry about what others think

Fall in and out of dancing with the storm

And dancing with the thought of being judged.

Funnily enough I wished I was alone

But I'd be invisible if I wasn't

The drops are like kisses

Soft kisses from the sky

Cradled in the midst of a power beyond control

Beyond prediction

Dangerous but safe

Embraced by thunder

Rain

Warmth

Even if we destroy everything

We can't destroy this

Heterochromia

RKP

They say your eyes are the window to your soul.

Does that mean I owe you these?   'Cos

She used to proudly say,

"That's mine & that's his."

Each belonging to what stuck in the marital bed,

Odd – just like their coupling.

Grey, slightly blue.

Hazel green.

Bullied for it after a classroom incident,

Asking Mrs Cooper, the Science teacher,

"Why?"

An eager year 10's hand reached up to catch

answers'n'explanations of mutations,

Never escaping decision making chromosomes.

I was doubly named freak, but this time of nature.

Pissed off parent peepholes perverted perceptions –

Damning my DNA in mirrors while white coloured balls stared back,

Begging Universe's symmetry,

"Make me blind."

If we are made by design,

Intricate movements dictated by higher powers…

Reflections of God's image,

How is he satisfied…with these?

That

Are

Not…

Reverse my blip of existence to utero.

Put holes where my being is two halves of their whole,

I don't want them anymore.

Looking Back

Kestral Gaian

Is it wrong to miss

what we no longer have?

Looking back to days gone by

When you're past the abyss,

and through all of the pain,

There was love that I could not deny.

I will feel it forever,

in this way and that,

as I think of him now and again,

I felt free as a feather -

but it wasn't forever,

and for months now I've had to abstain.

Moved on and smiling

we both seem to be,

and yet something will always be there

However, it's trying -

when the thought comes to me,

about how much we both used to care.

I hope they were true,

when they said that time heals

as I'm ready to give it a try,

I'm happy for you -

yet this is still how it feels,

looking back to days gone by.

Clickety clack

Kay Whitehurst

Clickety clack. Clickety clack

Clickety slack. Slickety back.

The wheels on the track, pulling everything back

The glorified stack on a man-made rack

Steel and stone and rotten wood pack

between the rails, that rumbling flack.

Heavy as a planet and 8 foot wide

Sparks of the engine in a power glide

Raindrops and snowdrops and hail sleet and sun

The driver atop his 200 tonnes

Moving the air as he powers along

Couldn't be much more focused if he tried

Hydraulics and pneumatics, pinch hiss and punch

Friction and braking and pulling with grunt

The beast in its lair, with a grin on its front

Of the menacing hulk of the gleaming red spring

Coiled from one end to the back of beyond

Potions for motion caused to career headlong

Into the wilderness pylon by pylon

Tricking the track, and splitting the flap

Of birds in mid-flight and swans on their nests

The wonder of modern technology bests

All things with four legs

But is it the best?

Clickety clack and clackety click,

The noises are nought short of deadening quick

Like the rain on the lake, taking motion to brace

Silence and comfort not even a thought

Though gone in four seconds, not leaving a trace.

Leaves rustle up to the cold winter air

Slamming back down when the gorgon comes near

Then rising again in a whirlwind of haste

And flying right off into the estate

Lights dim and horns blare the distracting whim

Of a journey so tactile it will suck you in

Clackety Click and tickety tack…

Onwards we fly and there's no turning back.

Matilda.

RKP

I'm argumentative,

Defiance, the defensive.

Is this assessed?

''No...''

I don't care about the room,

We haven't even begun,

Her wrong move – assumption.

Sorry, no, nothing all you say is wrong,

I just don't know you from Adam.

Do your homework- read my file.

Step down, step down.

Political stigmas and their pedestals,

Your tangents,

My confusion.

Articulate before the trigger, I'm down.

Crowned and bowing, you're a puppeted clown owned.

She's asking me a question,

I pause and gulp,

Almost swallowing my tongue,

Digesting the patronisation,

Her auto pilot robot explanation…

Mmm…

The sound behind her intention,

And the scratch of her pen,

Scribbles of not so secret sins,

I don't want to say it all,

Picked up and put down,

Again.

One small step - a song*

Ash Brockwell

I'm taking this one small step beyond the world I know,

Today I will reach a place I've never dared to go,

And I just don't care what people say,

I'm gonna feel the fear and do it anyway:

I'm taking that one small step that lets my passion grow…

Because life was meant for living, for exploring and forgiving,

Doesn't matter if they call me mad or weird or strange:

For I may never get another chance

to join this wild and crazy dance,

I can't keep waiting around for someone else to change!

I'm taking this one small step that brings my soul alive,

With barriers breaking down, my heart's in overdrive,

Don't you tell me that it can't be done,

'Cause I will not give up before I have begun:

I'm taking that one small step, just watch me learn to thrive!

I'm taking that one small step: oh, can you understand?

On days when I don't feel brave, will you please hold my hand?

Will you show me that I'm not alone,

And will you find a step that you can call your own?

For when we step up together, we can change this land!

Because life was meant for living, for exploring and forgiving,

Doesn't matter if they call us mad or weird or strange:

For we may never get another chance

to join this wild and crazy dance,

We can't keep waiting around for someone else to change!

* From 'TransVerse' exhibition, 2019:
www.ashbrockwell.com/transverse/small-step

Simply Beautiful

Kestral Gaian

Love is confusing.

Not love for God,

which is always simply beautiful,

but love for people.

Old love, that re-ignites when

you see someone again,

for the first time,

in years.

New love, all mixed up

with emotion.

Silent love - love you can

never admit.

Sometimes I think,

if man just loved God alone,

life would be much simpler.

But then, that would deny

our very human nature -

God meant for us to fall in love,

I believe. And love can never,

never ever,

be wrong or bad

Coder

Kay Whitehurst

Tippy tappy tapping. I type my life away.

My brains and memories wracking

To find the right array

Modules, methods, functions. I've coded in them all

I've often felt how proud I am, to have made them very small.

Connect to git, the green lights lit, the database hydrates

On my local cloud machine, to save on transfer rates.

My monstrous IDE is a tremendous sight to see

With autofill intellisense and plugins wild and free.

It finds the built-in methods and gives it to you straight

It sucks you in and eats your time and keeps you working late.

My code is quite the picture, it comments for itself

But if you ask me what I've done, I never can quite tell.

Did I cast that string into that array, or did I leave it hanging there?

Did I parse that date to an ISO, or did I leave it plain and bare?

For the full-bore job of a coder is very rarely done,

And the hero never gets their chance to wallow in the sun.

Do What Simon Says.

RKP

I was told once that you shouldn't play with angels,

They have the tendency to rip off halos,

N'use them for Frisbees.

Relationships floated like butterflies,

They stung like bees.

I'm just that bottom feeder,

Drips'n'table crumbs fed me,

So don't you go wavin' your finger,

I'm still squeaky clean'n'on Simon's best behaviour.

Some say I'm the meanest,

Honest, I'm organically the greenest…

My spliffs will make you swim with the fishes,

N'you'll see stars with all those wasted wishes.

Gots third eyes like satellite dishes.

I am dilated, diluted, and dislocated,

Herbalist Hish Grade specialist imported medications –

Mediate the mediations,

Rizla spittin' preparations,

Sober talkin'

Sober walkin'

Come on, watch me do my ABC's backwards…

Z

Y

X

W

V

U

T

…Shit my mind needs fumigating,

Febreeze it or something, Trust though I ain't into quittin' –

I'm a Bull on parade bleeding for you,

Do ya need the haemoglobin?

Emo violin respondin',

Strap me up.

Gimme an overdose'o'serotonin worth some grinnin',

Intravenously surfin' blood streaming'n'searching for happy.

The reminiscing rebelling Hippy with only the best intentions…

-   EST 1990 –

Nomadic by birth right,

In a hometown that breeds hindsights bitches.

Broken families'n'divorces forced fears and phobias,

Drivin' foolish feet forwards,

You'd find me hidden against old faux exteriors

of a county's academia,

Holding faith in sketchbook Bibles,

Skin held together by ring binders,

Stinkin' of acrylic that kept me alive,

Sniffin' back globs of chemicals called courage,

And from rigid ribs my lungs would exhale calm,

Skeletal smokin' in the belly of the Whale.

Filtering life's plankton,

N'armed with a sour tongue so sharp leaving toxic people

a half of what they once were,

Cos…

Didn't you see how fast they lied when those paddy wagons zoomed

'round that cul-de-sac corner?

Sticks & Stones are my bones so don't go tossin' them

over bridges of gas lit water…

I'll rebuild in emancipated streetlight glowing corners,

Licked by the brink of homeless flames,

I can – I am able.

I'll resist those words,

''It's not my problem'' – so flammable.

See my broken bricks still drip something untameable,

Resisting nerves,

Unswallowable,

Stomach churnable,

Can you make these words digestable?

Or into tears so pleasurable,

Tears of pain,

Both trickle the same – so colourful.

Like Emin's tent I'll write it down for you,

Then burn'n'boil it down to glue.

Don't drop that soap,

N'touch your toes,

Take a pich of kitchen sale,

N'toss over shoulders for the luck that held your innocence close,

Sing in tune to eclectic birdsong at dusk –

Chords for all those hymen hymns for all those parts

I do not know how to miss,

Listen can you hear my inner longing prayer

to a God that no longer exists?

Sit back,I'll tell ya some stories,

That ain't a sob, but a witnessed whimper,

Of survival & instinctual kick in's that kept

A 4 year old's, "Why Dad?" a whisper.

Musings of a tired mind

Kay Whitehurst

In restless sleep we dream our own

relentless thoughts and fears and so

we slumber less and writhe in stress

until the burden freed and

finally we sleep so deep

our tired souls to feed

Hair

Kay Whitehurst

Hair, hair, everywhere

In my eyes and in the air,

blowing out with auburn flair

in the glowing morning sun.

See not split ends, or knotted weave:

a sheet of silky bends and heaves

a sigh of pure relief, to be

free as the morning sun.

Meditation

Kay Whitehurst

sheets of gold and red lap quietly

at the shores of the horizon

waves of velvet colour roll slowly and quietly

over the hills and valleys

a lengthening shadow moves its way

across the resting countryside

and settles into the cracks and crevices

smells of cut grass, harvest pollen and roses

fill the evening air

the day, once in its vibrant glory,

seeming almost immortal,

breathes a sigh of heavy departure

and from the land, aromas and colours burst forth

filling the senses

 and ensnaring the mind.

Captivated,

I sit beside a crystal lake.

The colours around reflect in the calm waters below,

jumping slightly as a fish bobs to the surface

creating a shallow ripple which extends

beyond the reach of mankind.

I watch the canvas bleed the colours

slowly into each other,

as the evening draws on.

The candle flame beside me

grows ever more pronounced

against the purple, and eventually the black

of the night

as the last golden rays shoot heavenward from the burning sunset.

And as the night begins,

silence surrounds.

A tranquility so serene

that one could almost be wrapped in it.

A silence which makes the ears

believe that they are muted.

The stars shine in an endless inky sky,

the swirling wisps of cloud

wreath them and keep them.

The flame atop its waxy mantle

sputters and jumps in the warm summer breeze,

as the tendrils of the equatorial winds

ease over the land.

A wave of bright slumber comes across me as I sit,

the grass between my fingers and the cool water at my feet.

And I lean backwards, each lapping wave taking me further

into a land of dreams.

Each part of my body relaxes,

from the tips of my toes, moving like a blanket up my body,

and finally reaching my brain,

like being submerged into a pool of pure happiness.

And so my soul floats into the ether,

dragging along nothing of my cares or my worries.

It soars into the magnificent blackness,

through a portal which only I know.

Bliss.

Don't touch my hair

Frogb0i

I am not 'exotic'

I am not 'half cast'

I am not a 'chocolate man'

I am not 'the shade you want to go'

I am not a 'caramel latte'

I am not your 'token black friend'

I am not a 'US murder statistic waiting to happen'

My colour is irrelevant

My hair is irrelevant

My soil coloured eyes are irrelevant

My genetic background is irrelevant

Don't touch my hair

Road Rage

Kay Whitehurst

'Come friendly bombs and fall on Slough! / It isn't fit for humans now' –
from 'Slough' by John Betjeman

"Don't you ever use your indicators?"

Bleat the fuming raged commuters

Blink and beep and crash and clash

and sharpened tongues and shaking fists

The stinking bloated fat cat rides

with Range Rover Sport fetishists

Who skipped the bombs that fell on Slough

Who've never been off-road, and now

the diesel burns and tempers rage,

Brake lights, face and fuel gauge

Scarlet red and uncompromising, in this

Dead hearted cruel world surviving. Just.

And on to the future electric whizz,

the Tesla I-Y-whatever-it-is,

and where it comes from, no-one cares,

so long as it burns rubber, who dares?

to challenge it, their souls will bare

against the whittled spears.

Society rears, and turns its back,

not even now to cut it slack, it takes its place

in the stinking queue of fumes and hate

to suffer at the very same fate as

All the others stuck in time.

A tapestry of humanity, sublime?

Stuck motionless, oceanless, emotionless and sad.

Hats off to the stinking cad.

Rest in Peace.

Social Status

Rae-Lien Blais

Social media is an asshole

Leaves our mind an unfilled whole

Constantly nagging like a wondering troll

Leaves us all paying that toll

All the bs this crazy world unfolds

Never know which ways the balls will roll

Our minds begin to unfold

Our hearts start to pay the price

This world isn't nice

Social media is an asshole

Our hearts pay the taxes

Media determines will we sleep at night

This crap is whack

It isn't right

Take a look we are all up at night

I could be sleeping

Instead on this thing we call media

I be creeping

Needing to see who is up with me

Laying awake skimming

Like me wanting to find sleep

Social media is an asshole

Captures us

Carries us in too deep

Mountains too high

Never reaching the peak

Wondering

Who is next to speak

Texting is all we see

Communication is lost

Words we do not see

Nothing from our lips

Just media you see

Social media is an asshole

Attacks living beings

Like you

And me

Words cut short

Grammar out of sorts

Social media's an asshole

Tears us down one by one

Just when you think you're done

Social media

Again you have ONE

Social media is an asshole

Yeah we still have call waiting

Instead we sit by our phones debating

Do we answer

Do we sit debating

Do we sit waiting for the phone to stop ringing

Talking to a friend while the iPhone is ringing

No running home to make a call

Children at school walking through the halls

Phones in their ears

Not afraid to be caught

With gum in mouths popping

Instead telling the principal to stop

On the phones they are talking

Sitting in classes making a call

Texting while a teacher calls their name

Telling them to hold

Social media is more important than the world we live in

No more memorable dinners at the table with family

Just seeing what is up on FB twitter or instagram

How was school today

It was good

I texted my friend on FB

OH I posted a selfie

Can I get new headphones mine broke

See this shit media is a JOKE

A conversation cannot last more than a minute

Without can I play on your tablet or a text that was given

What would have happened if this was the first century

No flat screens computers or smart phones you see

No laptops no google or ipods or yoohoo wait yahoo

Do you see how much we can get from a day

If social media just went away

So what you children have iphones

Some that don't

Know how to unlock a phone at JUST three years old

You do not know where your children are so you call them

Still we chose when to answer

This social media is a CANCER

Killing us off like a really bad dancer

Teaching kids how to post their goods

Twelve years olds is this really good

Sitting around we wait for a text

Wondering what a person will say next

What happen to coming home when the street lights came on

NOPE

Just another text from a child to mom

Can I stay out

I won't be late

See we are on face book trying for plans to make

This social media we count on is a loaded gun

Killing us off one by one

Paedophiles hiding behind a screen

Pretending to be a Brett or Dean

Isn't that mean

Kidnapping a child who thinks they are grown

All because on social media their parents made a choice

to let them roam

Social media is an asshole

You see it attacks everyone

You and me

I fall guilty

See I fall prey

To the evil media that exists today

Social media is an asshole

This isn't done

See social media

Do we not see it again

Has ONE

Do we not see the social media that we use is a scam

Constantly putting us all in a jam

What happened to a simple way

INSTEAD we are spoiled

Again we stray from the wonders of today

The pleasure in life

To see what next will disturb our life

Social media is a terrible game that is NEVER done

See because tonight

  Social media again has ONE

Three a.m. again

Where am I again

Wish I would just fall into REM

Not going to happen

Media's got you friend

Worst enemy you see

Pulled me down again

NO sleep you see

This place you think is your friend

your mind has been deceived

TW: Downward spirals

The World Health Organisation finally confirmed in 2018 that being transgender is not a mental illness. However, in the face of dysphoria, misgendering, deadnaming, media hostility, fear of abuse, rejection by family members, and often the loss of friends to suicide or murder, it's hardly surprising that the trans community has a high rate of mental health problems.

Poetry, along with other forms of art, can give us a safe outlet for intense feelings of grief, self-loathing and hopelessness. We often write them just for ourselves as a form of release, hoping that putting them into words and capturing them on a page might stop them from swirling around endlessly and wordlessly in our minds. But when we do share them, it's usually in the hope of finding solidarity, not sympathy – reaching out to discover whether someone out there might feel the same, to prove that we're not truly alone in a vast dark universe.

The fact that you're reading these poems is proof that what might feel like the end of everything, in this moment, doesn't have to *be* the end of everything. Some of them were written by people who couldn't see a way forward at that point; but they found the strength within them to stay alive.

While you might have to wait for the next chapter to find the glimmer of hope, for now it's enough to know it exists.

Specific trigger warnings for poems in this chapter are as follows:

Title	Page	Author	Theme(s)
Caroline	147	Frogb0i	Anxiety, panic attacks, therapy
The spiral	148	Kay Whitehurst	Depression, suicidal thoughts
My life in hell	151	AJ	Anxiety, depression, rejection, self-harm
If it fits	156	RKP	Childhood abuse, suicidal thoughts
Dark angel	158	Kay Whitehurst	Depression
Chain mail	160	RKP	Death, grief, childhood abuse
To be Free`	164	Kay Whitehurst	Depression, self-harm
Trans*	165	Megan Nightingale	Depression, transphobia, suicidal thoughts
End of the line	166	RKP	Abuse, depression, suicidal thoughts

Caroline

Frogb0i

Who is Caroline?

I go to her with my problems

and she stores them up like a floppy disk.

remember those?

I give them to her and they are no longer mine.

I give them to her and I don't have a panic attack.

I don't have a panic attack on the bus

that the cis white man is staring at my crotch.

I let them pour out of me and it feels like

when you are unexpectedly caught in the rain.

You are caught in the rain in a t-shirt from the night before,

and remember that you haven't slept in your own bed in a while.

The spiral

Kay Whitehurst

Slip sliding downwards, a well of bleak oppression

Sucking every facet from your existence

The broken hands of a faded clock tick

Heavily in the dark

Swallowed hard in the gullet of a dying whale

Through the sands of every time imaginable

I drown. I take it all with graciousness

It is all I deserve and all I am due

Staring down the barrel of a gun and wishing I had the balls

To pull the trigger and make it end, but my balls were

Taken years ago.

Killing screams in the dead of night.

Death squared in the root of evil

We crawl like ants on the face of the earth

And our lives begin and end

Silently

Purposeless

On the cold slab of a mortuary of dirt.

Staring at the blurred edges of the fractured sky

Death approaches on raven wings and circles

Making waves and patterns in the cloud

Above my head. Wish we were dead

Killing fields in the ceasefire of the heart

I climbed out of the mud too many years ago

I clawed at the edges of reason

I made no sense of the devil's spawn

But he collared me for treason

Insane in the brain, like the rain

On the plain abandoned site

Of the primordial existence of pain

Crawling in our filth we foreshadow the truth

A thousand suns burning the earth to ash.

Spirals within spirals for a billion years

Aching for the end of an engorged society

Fat with greed on the edge of a knife

Civilization curls into dust

Like the heat of a lamp withers a flower

Bring down the might of a supernova

Tear away the flesh and hollow the bone

Gone in a blink of an eye forever.

We die a husk of ourselves

Emptied and void of the life we once possessed

What is the point of this life?

We cannot get out alive, we just

Propagating the species and continuing the lie

What are our options? Who should we be?

Drowning in the pool of tears

And the Black hole spirals again.

Death becomes me

My life in hell

AJ

When I think someone cares
And then they don't, it flares
All I do is try
But instead I cry

When I think I'm flying
But realise that I'm dying
Some say think big
But what about thinking small

When people are around they don't pay attention.
When I'm crying, they don't even mention
They look at me in normality
But then, they don't in reality

They know I have anxiety
But they still make a big group society
There's no one around to talk
And when there is, they say "go for a walk"

Everyone hates me

Then I count to three

Everyone leaves and disappears

But that's fine, I've been alone for years

Loving someone kills

But staying with them is the pills

Even the person you love wants more

But it feels just like a chore

Trying to find money

To go see my honey

But he lives too far away

So I think of him beside me every day

I wish I died

So you don't know things I go through inside

When I die

You seem to fly

I don't know what I would do if you weren't here

I think I would've just had a beer

I'd get so drunk

Then you'd say something and my heart sunk

Spend all my time on my own
Then I talk to people on my phone
People don't like the way I look
So I hide myself in a book

I can't read
And my eyes bleed
When you think you're in love
Then they tell me from above

When loving someone it's hard
But losing someone it bared
When missing someone it hurt
So that's why I took your shirt

You can't see my scars
When you are looking at the stars
I'm feeling used
And I'm getting abused

Why love someone when you love someone more

And that someone I adore

Emo I know

But i'm still in love with him though

Why fall in love when you know it's going to end

So then I ask, `can I just be your friend?

Later he wants me back and I say,

`I am going away!'

I put all my trust

Then it gets bust

Then I was gone

So I mowed the lawn

Finding love

Is trying to find a lost glove

Hurting myself every day

Keeping the demons at bay

Drowning in blood

Like you're playing stuck in the mud

I have scars

But you can't see when I'm behind bars

When you thought you'd never get your smile back

And then your heart goes black

When someone comes back to life

Then you drop the knife

All is well

When I'm coming out of my shell

But when I think someone cares

And then they don't, it flares...

If it fits.

RKP

Silence & smiles are my worst enemy,

So loud.

But what happens between these four walls,

Does not leave these four walls.

Unnatural habitats.

Emotional vibrations are tangible,

No guiding hands, just screwdrivers in elastic bands.

Dark coloured conversations are vicious,

Marking silver skins black and blue.

Parental disciplines,

Tauntingly testin'n'tantilizing my brain.

I have feral roots in my spine,

Family branches are dead.

We were brought up like pit bulls –

Played against each other.

3's a crowd – no ring, just a house.

N'when you lose you're in that corner,

Rocking backwards and forwards,

Mother's milk must have been poison.

Are there strings in my palms?

Or just a tailored blame that fits me now?

I still don't know why I did it…

Ask me what I'm proud of…

Nothing.

Euthanise me.

She used to say,

"If they hit you, hit back ten times harder…"

Just like she did,

'Cos life don't give you what you can't handle.

Dark angel

Kay Whitehurst

A dark decaying forest lies malevolently ahead,
its cerebral ghosts of twisted lives past, collude
in a pall of morbid self-indulgence.
As prophets and martyrs look on from their pillars
of salt, and know not how unsteady is their foundation.

Dark eyed and pilloried, a raven cast angel, this
angel, draws close to the ebony night
And runs her fingers through rotten flowers where
once a thriving garden grew.

Her fears, your fears, ring there – A shadowy
flight into a world so dark and twisted, that
it makes death seem a joyous occasion.
She turns, eyes glazed black, a spectral cloak
of mist surrounding her as she glares at nothingness,
slowly being eroded by the fetid tendrils of time.

A painted world of shadows, dark fleeting
glimpses into the minds of the dead – souls of
poets, painters, writers, sadists and politicians. Every
single one a portent of the oncoming storm,
the apocalypse of mankind.

The grave guards of the land will awaken, driven by the
tears of the damned, black pools of stinking flesh,
cried out and squeezed from the acrid smoke of the end of life.
A world burns, the screams of the dying reach out
Into the night, starless, cold, unwavering in the
certainty of extinction.

The angel watches on, fixed, transfixed, her gaze
melting the façade of life.

Chain mail.

RKP

Dead'n'buried,

She's had her burial.

N'the regret you feel, is what she always wanted.

6 foot under your feet,

Her promise of pain,

Abortions – Knitting needles,

You probably guilt tripped the priest,

Her flowers putrid'n'rotting off the wreath.

The head stone like her heartbeats,

Now a head board,

No rest,

No peace,

Please, as she gazes towards the eastern horizon.

May she turn, and turn in that hole.

May she not rise with us again.

This death was her apology.

N'I know it's the common tongue,

But this silence IS killing me.

You and I we've cut out another line,

The funeral.

An epitaph – monumental memory,

The mother without her children,

Playing the victim,

Pause as you hum the marches note,

"My daughter the black scapegoat",

Not a sheep, can't be herded or controlled.

That's it, I'm to blame, pass the fault,

Sing you hymns, smell those roses, through tinted glasses,

Blacked out with grief at the wake but,

You missed out all their names.

It bleeds, she said, like her heart,

Her twist of history resurfaced,

A metaphor – my skin,

My sins.

Trials, terrors, my errors, saying she knows my pain,

The quiet violence that leaves me shivering,

Creeping through my veins,

My poltergeist plays with my feelins,

Like growing pains,

Nature verses nurture,

Growing traumas.

"Our parents just love us in different ways."

He loves it when I say that.

I creak,

And I'm aching,

I am tiring of this.

My boundary is now the skyline,

Back to back,

The space,

Stay there,

The distance, in between.

I'll keep running this time,

Whilst you stand there stuck in time

Hoping like I did.

Voiceless messages letting me know,

You're still alive and kicking.

Stolen from on going chains,

Emptiness in the stillness,

In your living room filled with tears,

Surrounded by photos of those who no longer visit,

An empty response.

Yet, I imagine you are moved by the words,

"Merry Christmas!

I start with you…

Now you're on the clock.

In 9 minutes something will make you happy.

Please share this with 15 friends you love.

If I don't get this back I'm obviously not a close friend.

Once you've read this, you have to send it to 15.

It's not that hard.

Whoever sent this to you must care about you."

Hang on, are we missing something?

To Be Free

Kay Whitehurst

You feel the caress, skin on skin

Letting your demons in, throwing the light to shade

And being remade in the essence of your love.

Kissing the stone, feeling alone

Was the only way you've ever really known

To exist inside your mind, now you find

It's impossible to go back, no matter how hard you try.

But still you get the downs, drive you out, drive you in

The devil within keeps you plucking at his whim

Like a solitary hero in a badly coloured film

Plucking away at the threads that keep you in

Feeling the cold of the blade on your skin

Start with a cut and it all begins to win

Fading away into your confinement of sin

Rivers of red that seem to drown out the din

Of your thoughts, of your fears, of your isolating years,

Placing burdens of guilt on your mind, and you find,

That these things pierce you like spears

To the core of your existence

But knowing who you are, who you love, is enough

To dig only surface deep, to save all your blood

Just the sensation of pain to keep your mind on the job

Of life and love and casting poverty off

Your thoughts are a maze, you keep them amazed,

With the tangle of notions inside

But when it comes to the grain, you own your own pain

And find that you can just about push it aside

For the one you love, and they pain they'd face

If they found that they could never have that final embrace.

If they had to live their life with just an empty space

You couldn't leave them hanging with only a trace of you.

Knife on skin and skin to bone,

We never want to be alone

To be cast out in this world of hatred, violence and greed

We need to cast off our skin and our home

To be Free.

Trans*

Megan Nightingale

Alone, I,

anxiously peruse the dating platform debris,

searching for, hoping for,

someone to love.

Trapped I sit,

within this dilapidated bedsit,

surrounded by violence and anger and noise,

longing to be free.

Seated in isolation, I exist as

a perceived perversion, a `dick in a dress',

anomalistic, outcasting others' understanding,

drenched in lethargy.

Suicidal, I

brave the crowds between, a bistro and me,

seeking refuge from a cis-het storm and,

avoiding the inevitable evening pain.

End of the line

RKP

Promises hang like cigarettes,

The dance like shadows on walls,

Disappearing when that unhopeful light draws closer.

This tempo is unclean…

The bas is eating…

What do you want with a Devil like me?

Fancy some shameful company?

Called a clever chameleon, see,

Easily mouldable,

Budging the rules,

What you gonna do about it?

That's it – nothing at all.

Don't swear to God, he didn't ask ya,

Prayer is dank breathe on the air,

N.my roar is that creak in your door,

As you creep along the floor to turn the light off…

"Not in."

"Don't answer."

"There's no room in the inn."

N'all Mother says is,

"Oh dear, well I gotta go cos m'tablets are kickin' in."

Weak link feeling.

Loyal blood runs cold in this family,

This pedigree ain't sound,

Ancestral abuse stops with me,

Make good of the prison – your home.

Jail bars quiver anxiously,

Skin up, breathe out,

Accepting mind-set – I'm alone,

We're alone.

Did you know

there's a supermassive black hole slowly sucking us down?

Let the pressure take and fold.

The Milky – Way is a dark cloudy Monday.

Beginning just to end.

Is this to exist, no presence?

'Cos we'll be gone in the blink of your baby's existence –

It's a different politic,

Queer perceptions,

Conspiracal speculations,

Thoughts drip outta me like wet cakes,

Voices push past colour like supernovas,

Oh Father, Oh Father leave my frontal lobal, grab Jeu Jeu's tool.

There's no point...

Tune in, turn off, drop out, drop the remote.

Fancy readin' an 11yr olds social report?

They're stuck,

We forget that rabbit lights throw ya.

Here we go again...

You're plugged in to the troubles of a loser.

You'd see the reality – what they did to me.

If our bodies weren't healers...

All the bruises, all the lines.

"Love Bleeds."

An evil eye, nostrils'n'lungs – I'm ugly.

No features, just middle man numbers.

Would you meet me at the gates –

A bothersome burdened black tarred'n'feathered soul?

Do you think they'd call out my names?

Count your piggies.

Cross your digits.

Thoughts of those branches carrying me lingers,

Dead bodies like pendulums.

I carry pain like it's currency,

History is messy,

Paying for it daily,

Eating mud 3 squares a day,

Never moving, forever falling,

Down the hole I dug cos I just couldn't stop saying sorry.

Finding hope

While poetry can give us an outlet for negative thoughts, it can also lead us back to hope. The poems in this chapter aren't guaranteed to be free of triggering content, but they all end on a high note – celebrating the strength, resilience, pride and solidarity of the trans community.

On our better days, we recognise our transness as a gift, not a curse. We remember that for thousands of years, trans people have been (and, in some places, still are) honoured and celebrated for their ability to cross boundaries, question norms and see things differently. We might be living in difficult times and places right now, but that doesn't mean that it's always been that way, nor that it always will.

On our better days, we can look in the mirror and love what we see – or at least *imagine* a day when we'll be able to.

Trans Lives, Trans World

Vanilla (Refugee Trans Initiative)

trans lives

trans world

my beautiful trans dress and hair

and all the colourful make-up

and beauty full with love

that comes with it…

we will not be erased!

We Shine On

Emily (Refugee Trans Initiative)

trans women are beautiful

and a source of light

to the community

and the world at large...

our Light

we shine on!

Ancient Shore

Kay Whitehurst

Fading away at the end of the day
like an old distant beggar all alone
like the lipstick stain lingers on the rim of a glass
like the moss-covered boulder or stone
And the song it sings on in the warm setting sun
singing sweetly to carry us home.

So we curtsy and bow to the orchestra high,
to our family and friends gone before
As we close tight our eyes and give up a sigh
we wash up on that old ancient shore
where our ancestors trod, and into this land
they gave themselves up evermore.

So sleep on, little darling, sleep on,
Dream sweetly of oceans and waves,
Let the wonders you seek find you there in your mind
and take you to long-distant caves,
for when you're asleep the real world stops,
and the hurt is temporarily erased.

Timeless Story - a song

Ash Brockwell

Light me a candle and tell me a timeless story,

Whisper your dreams of the world you long to see;

Now, as the nights grow long,

let love and friendship keep us strong, and

Come share a tale by the fireside with me!

Talk about the roads you've travelled,

talk about the sun and rain,

All the insights and the mysteries,

all the joy and all the pain,

Talk about the times you never

quite believed you'd make it through,

And the days when you remembered

no-one else is quite like you.

Tell me when you woke and realised

life would never be the same,

Tell me when you owned the struggle,

tell me when you learned your name.

Tell me how you found your power,
how you faced your greatest fears,
How the vision deep within you
grew and strengthened through the years.

Light me a candle and tell me a timeless story,
Whisper your dreams of the world you long to see;
Now, as the nights grow long,
let love and friendship keep us strong, and
Come share a tale by the fireside with me!

All the names the haters called you,
all the words that left a scar,
All the masks you cast aside to
face the world as who you are,

All the times you lived your vision,
made your friends and loved ones proud,
All the times you stood for justice,
dared to speak your truth aloud.

May these tales of pain and victory,

told in prose or sung in rhyme,

Lift our spirits in the darkness

as we weave the web of time;

As the wheel of life keeps turning

with each cycle of the moon,

Still the candle keeps on burning:

brighter days will be here soon!

Light me a candle and tell me a timeless story,

Whisper your dreams of the world you long to see;

Now, as the nights grow long,

let love and friendship keep us strong, and

Come share a tale by the fireside with me!

* From 'TransVerse' exhibition, 2019:
www.ashbrockwell.com/transverse/timeless-story

Love Conquers All

Tina Cross

We're born, we grow, we learn, we live.

Some learn to hate, some to forgive.

Love conquers all, or so they say

But it takes time, not just one day.

From tiny acorns oak trees grow

Love is the message we should sow

Some battles lost, but wars to win

Every loss grows strength within

Religion, gender, colour of skin

Targets all for hatred's whim

Make love shine, like a summer sun

Hold out your hand and live as one

Gentle breezes may start to blow

But into storms they soon may grow

It's up to us just how we live:

Don't learn hate, but to forgive.

The Valley

Bingo Allison

This valley between two heights
Was once verdant and green
A garden of earthly delights
Sadly now rarely seen

And God walked in the cool of this garden
Loving the joys he had made
Touching and tasting everything that grew
Colours of light and of shade

But there was a war in creation
That broke the Creator's heart
Nation rose against nation
And tore the valley apart

The victors drew up on one of the peaks
And declared themselves lords ever after
The losers they sent to the opposite side
To work and to toil for their masters

The rulers called themselves "men"
And they were all that was good
And everything servile was "woe-men"
Under rules the men understood

The rules drew all of the wonder
From the valley into the two hills
Variety rent asunder
Withering under their will

And life was drained from the valley
Everything sadness and loss
Analogue into binary
With nothing permitted to cross

Years went by and the Creator mourned
For the flourishing of Their toil
Weeping and wailing, tear upon tear
Falling on dry, dusty soil

And the waters welled up in the desert
Making rivers and streams in the plain
And colour returned to that which was burned
Things that had died grew again

Some on the hills most intrepid
Whose life there had never quite fit
Began to make their home in the vale
Others deciding to cross it

There are many now moving and changing
Blessing and filling the land
But many on the hills are complaining
They're breaking the rules of the man

But we are children of the Creator
Who delights beyond woman and man
Who makes life spring up in the desert
And loves all that's unique in the land

So wherever you live in the valley
From wherever you walked to be free
God will clear your skin and water your crops
Bless life nonbinary

In the Sky

Marcus Pabon-Lara

In the sunset

Walk through the forest

By the trees

Look at the orange mist in the sky

I know it will be very special tonight

At night

Look up at a load of sparkling stars in the sky

Looking at them is one of my favourite hobbies

It is always a fantasy to me.

I wonder if stars are angels

They always look down at us

Granting our wishes

Stars are like our dreams

Make our dreams come true

The world a better and brighter

Place for me and you

When I try to reach the stars

It gives me hope

What my future may hold

Let my aspiration unfold for me too!

The Flame - a song

Ash Brockwell

When the pain becomes too much for me to bear,

When I cry aloud for help, but no-one's there,

When the path is long and steep, and there's no-one as my guide,

I become the Flame; I light the Flame inside!

I am not this body, I am not this pain,

I am not extinguished by endless storms and rain,

You can hate me or despise me, but you can't put out my light,

I am the Flame: I'll keep on burning bright!

I am not the mourner paralysed by loss,

I am not the ego that longs to be the boss,

I am not that hollow loneliness that yearns for someone's kiss,

I am the Flame: I'm so much more than this!

I am not the stories that I used to tell,

Problems, drama, trauma, and feeling so unwell,

I am not the helpless victim who does nothing but endure,

I am the Flame: I'm truly so much more!

When the pain becomes too much for us to bear,

When we cry aloud for help, but no-one's there,

When the path is long and steep, and there's no-one as our guide,

We become the Flame; we light the Flame inside!

Let your heart remember what it's always known,

Feel the fire within you, and know you're not alone,

We will forge a new community, ignite the healing ways,

We are the Flame: let's set the world ablaze!

* From 'TransVerse' exhibition, 2019:

www.ashbrockwell.com/transverse/the-flame

Bad Light

Kestral Gaian

We say "it's bad light" when we don't love,

The vibrancy of the colours of the world above.

We photoshop everything, We fake, and we fudge.

But things look okay,

By the light of day.

We cover our skin in oils and in paints,

Convinced we must make ourselves look more like saints.

We butcher, Inject, Remodel and Taint.

But things look alright,

In natural light.

We have this most unnatural notion,

All of these plans that we must set in motion,

Size zero, image, obsession, devotion.

But how great things seem,

With a natural gleam.

I weep when I think that this is how we raise,

A whole generation to behave.

We're unique creatures, not fashion slaves.

And we all look okay,

By the light of day.

You Are Enough

Ash Brockwell

To that person

…who Googles 'transgender' when everyone's in bed

…who's always felt weird and wrong and a failure

…who stares longingly at the clothes they aren't ready to buy

…whose parents will never, ever call them by their chosen name

…whose parents just threw them out on the street

…who had to smile sweetly while a customer verbally abused them

…who can't take one more transphobic headline

…who's still figuring out what their gender is

…whose gender doesn't even have a name

…who's been waiting more than two years for their first appointment

…who wishes they could just do the surgery themselves

…who's struggling with the side-effects of treatment

…who will never be able to get the treatment they need

…who's still getting misgendered after all these years

…who's still getting flashbacks after a violent attack

…who can't even tell their best friend because they won't get it

…who believes they'll never find ANYONE who gets it

…who believes they're the only person who ever felt this way

…who's just so done with everything and everyone

To that person
and all the others I haven't mentioned
this poem is for you

I want you to remember this:
there is nothing wrong with being trans
and there is no wrong way to be trans

on the days when dampness
seeps into your soul
staining your bright colours with mildew

on the days when half-remembered trauma
drowns your best intentions
in a flood of uninvited emotion

on the days when a grey fog
tangles itself around your mind
and distant neurons cry out desperately
for each other in a vain attempt
to reconstruct the list of unfinished tasks
and find a way to begin...

on THOSE days,

you know the ones…

I want you to write this on your fridge:

you are enough, even if you don't feel it

I want you to etch this into your mirror:

you are valid, even if you don't see it

I want you to tattoo this over your scars:

you are loved, even if you don't know it

* From 'TransVerse' exhibition, 2019:
www.ashbrockwell.com/transverse/you-are-enough

I was once like you

Kay Whitehurst

I was once like you, a shadow in a costume play

A dress rehearsal for an unknown show,

and you don't know your part

Like a feather on the gale force wind, swept away in the expectations

Carried on to unknown shores.

I was once like you, restless yearning in my heart

Desperate clawing for a person I knew I should have been

15 years old and scraping away the beauty of youth

The roughened edges of a broken soul

You may feel as I did, like running and never stopping

You may feel as I did, like your life's an empty glass

Waiting for the world to start, and for life to jump on board

For the earth and sky to straight align, and wake you up a girl.

But the time it knows no boundaries, and the heartache never lasts

The grey clouds hanging over you will clear with icy blast

You're more than just the sum of your parts,

And you can truly be you.

I was once like you, stealing dresses from my friends,

Hiding bras in the bottom of the wardrobe

and counting all the trends;

I fought to keep it secret and not reveal the sin

To lock the doors, keep out of sight, to keep the shame within.

I was once like you, throwing morals to the wind

Crossing every boundary just to be the girl within

Kleptomania for feminine wiles, and a habit carries on

Do you want her or want to be her? The confusion has begun

But the time flies by and frees you,

There's no such thing as too old

Your soul it drives and compels you

To fall into the fold

Theta your mind has been preparing,

Since the day that you were born

You can truly be yourself

Just leave the fears forlorn

Throw off your shadow, come into the light.

Never be shy to put up a fight
Tell the doctors you're you, face the family with pride
No longer do you have to put up and hide
Because I was once like you, but just look at me now
If I could go back 20 years, I'd explain how,
You can discard your anxiety, unburden your sin
The only thing sinful is keeping it in.

Be who you are, and the world will be here,
Waiting with smiles, big hugs and cheers
For they all know more now than they ever did
Acceptance is higher than it's ever been
Your time is right now and your place has been saved
We see you and love you. And respect that you're brave

I was once like you, but look at me now.
I am who I am, and my smiles know no bounds

Why Trans-Pride?

Paula Adrianne

Leeds holds a Pride event

In August of each year

A day for the LGBT

To raise a collective cheer

Many now have equal rights

And it fills my soul with glee

But some have been left behind

I'm talking about the T.

Not everyone can celebrate

We can't all 'Party On'

For some the fight continues

Our rights are not yet won

And when we do turn up to Pride

No one knows we're here

As press & TV erasure

Make trans-people disappear

But the trans of Leeds have had enough

We've found another way

So join us for Leeds Trans Pride

Held on TDOV day

It's a day to be visible

It's a day to make a fuss

A day for trans and enbies

To rejoice in being us

But it also is a protest

A challenge to all the TERFs*

A time for us to claim

Our rightful place on Earth

* TERF = 'Trans-Exclusionary Radical Feminists'

One Foot In Front Of The Other - a song

The Bleeding Obvious

I've yet to meet a person who hadn't been beat

By something someone did or said

There will be happy times ahead.

Sometimes it don't work out

You want to scream and shout

Were it easy to be you then life would be so untrue.

Take each day at a time

Soon the sun will shine

There's a hill you need to climb.

One foot in front of the other.

Take each day at a time

Soon the sun will shine

Life won't always be sublime

One foot in front of the other.

I've yet to learn of someone who didn't u-turn

Collateral along the road

In a big depressive episode.

And when it don't checkout,

Stop. Work it out.

Perhaps out of the blue they'll see a different side of you.

Take each day at a time

Soon the sun will shine

There's a hill you need to climb.

One foot in front of the other.

Take each day at a time

Soon the sun will shine

There's a hill you need to climb.

One foot in front of the other.

From the album 'Rainbow Heart':
http://bleedingobvious.uk/rainbowheart

On the other side of darkness - a song*

Ash Brockwell

When you're all alone, and you think you're breaking down,
And it seems the world's turned to shades of grey and brown,
And you're so damn tired of the pain and the confusion,
Know the only thing that's breaking down is illusion…

For on the other side of darkness there's a dawn where hope begins,
And on the other side of hatred there's a Love that always wins;
On the other side of winter we will light the Sacred Flame,
And by its light you'll find the people
who will call you by your name.

Know the stars still shine in the cloudiest of sky,
You can face your fears, don't pretend and don't deny,
When you look within, you become your own defender,
And the only way you'll make it through is surrender…

For on the other side of darkness there's a dawn where hope begins,
And on the other side of hatred there's a Love that always wins…

* From 'TransVerse' exhibition, 2019:
www.ashbrockwell.com/transverse/other-side

A butterfly prayer

Samantha Smith

For all our friends

Close and far

Living under the sun

Or in the sky with the stars

Do no wrong and patient be

This life is short for you and me

Find new friends and take a chance

Seeds of love in hearts we plant

Forgive the ones who have done us wrong

The light in them is dim not strong

Take courage in who you are

We are blessed & all made from the same star �֍

The Dawn of Trust

Kay Whitehurst

It is the fear which surrounds us, defines us and nearly drowns us
In the sea of the everyday, pulling and pushing life away
The sour air of lifetimes past comes rushing by at last

And so we see the curse of our mis-birth
and unfurl our true identity on this earth
The scenes of carnage in the past all fade away to black at last, and
Give birth to new views and new love and everything in between.

To the scene of lovers lost, a cause so just
in the eye of the mind's true Lust –
wandering in the cold for so many aeons past
and now finds form in the yellowing dusk.
The dawn of trust.

And when we admit that our old life was wrong,
that our true self lives on, in the pattering rain of the new day –
Then we see that we are nothing but free,
to be who we were meant to be
since that very first time we lay
on the earth, on the grass of this lifetime we pass,
and happily smile forever more.

Woman, Warrior, Queen

Queen Victoria Ortega

Men come up to me

they say hello and asks for my name

before I respond I remember the pain.

Memories of rejection and laughter.

I ask myself

do I answer

do I have a choice?

and I hope

he doesn't notice

 my deep voice

I answer "Queen Victoria"

and then they walk away saying "shit!"

 Angry at having been "fooled"

But fret I do not

for a shield and dagger I have tooled

They can't tell me what to do

How to look or how to sound

For by the binary – I am not bound.

I refuse to fake my voice and sound

like someone stuck a helium tube up my ass.

I am me

and that's that.

Do I sound different?

Do I look different?

Ya dam Skippy!

And I love myself for it.

That is my real strength

and our real strength of my community.

We Know that all the odds

are against us at this point in history,

my culture devalues trans women because we said –

fuck male privilege –

in order to live as our authentic selves.

We don't have job opportunities

nor access to trans affirm healthcare

we are not looked at as viable life partners

and shit

if we get real

I mean really real

 not even our gay lesbian and allies

know what to do with us

but why do we persist you ask?

– because we are so dam powerful

so so dam real, dam beautiful,

and so dam resilient

that we must show the rest of humanity

what the fuck it means

to personify the word

chingona

or

badass

see that is my story and my heritage

 I am Queen Victoria Elizabeth Marie Josephine Ortega

the Woman Warrior,

and the fucken Queen.

Hang On In There*

Ash Brockwell

Ignore them. Keep living. The world needs your breath.

Don't give them the pleasure of causing your death.

The world's full of haters: yes, that much is clear,

But the thing that annoys them is seeing us here,

So don't check out now, please. Stay here. Don't give in.

Let's keep on annoying them. Don't let them win.

Yes, I know that they've hurt you, and we're hurting too,

To see how they took out their anger on you:

They've ripped you to shreds and they've trashed all your days,

And you're stuck back together in very strange ways.

There's no way to go back and undo the harm,

But your crazy new shape has its own kind of charm.

The journey is long but you've travelled so far,

Fought so many fears to become who you are:

And yes, you're amazing. You'll say it's not true,

But there's someone out there who's inspired by you.

There's someone who sees you and loves what they see,

And thinks, 'Hey, one day maybe that will be me!'

It's OK to admit that you don't feel OK,

It's OK not to wash all the dishes today,

It's OK to sigh deeply and go back to bed

When you can't get away from the thoughts in your head;

But what isn't OK is to quit on us now:

Resolve to keep going, and soon you'll learn how.

The kids of the future will look back, bemused

At the way human beings were once so abused

For being themselves and for living their lives;

They'll admire the way that the spirit survives.

So come on. We've got this. The haters can't win.

Keep hanging on in there. Don't ever give in.

* From 'TransVerse' exhibition, 2019:
www.ashbrockwell.com/transverse/hate-crime

Facets

Megan Nightingale

The tandemonious transition:

one sat trepid of being shunned,

being different; diverse; unresolved,

whilst waiting to be transformed.

Reciprocal longing and non-refunded reputability,

respect given but not rewarded, instead,

faced with ridicule, seeking reprieve from,

incessant invection.

Archaic apathy:

arched to the plight of the atypical,

a lack of mutual assimilation to,

difference in experience.

Nonchalance of elitists,

as based upon nomotheticism, alien ineptness to,

the trans* plight, neglect of non-binary,

a refusal to validify.

Strength:

held by trans* residing in solitude,

stoically persevering through each day, steadfast,

inspirational, secure in their self-worth.

Shine

Kestral Gaian

People will stare
as you step into the limelight,
A shining example
of beauty and brain.

People will cheer
with you and for you,
At every corner
and round every turn.

People will smile
as they see all the things,
that you can do
and you can achieve.

People will wish
through jealous eyes,
that they could be there
doing what you do.

Now is the start,

it's all ahead

but all so easy

to grasp.

People don't know

just how bright

you can really

shine.

Semicolon*

Ash Brockwell

My sentence does not end here;

it goes on. I feared I couldn't do this;

I was wrong. I thought I'd been extinguished;

yet a white-hot ember burns. I felt my radiance fading;

but your love, my oxygen, revives me, and the flame of hope returns;

another second, one more minute, one more hour;

even one more day? My story is not over, this is all I know;

the power of my heart may yet sustain this glow. The spiral spins;

the sun begins to rise, its soft light lifts me from my 3a.m. despair;

my breath is in its care. The sentence is reduced to life, not death;

my story will continue, my beloved friend, for this is not the end;

* From 'TransVerse' exhibition, 2019:
www.ashbrockwell.com/transverse/semicolon

Thank you for reading our poems and sharing our journeys.

We may have stood on the edge and stared into the void; but we're still here.

We might be left with scars, visible or invisible; but we are survivors.

We are transgender and/or non-binary, and we march on with pride.

#TransPeopleArePeople

#WeWontBeErased

#PoetryIsPower

Our stories go on;

In love and solidarity,

Aidan, AJ, Alex, Andi, Ash, Bingo, Devin, Emily, Frogb0i, Jani, Jon/Joan, Julie, Kay, Kestral, Kim, Marcus, Megan, Paula, Queen Victoria, Rae-Lien, RKP, Samantha, The Bleeding Obvious, Tina, Tyler and Vanilla

List of Contributors

Aidan Sarson (he/him): I'm a trans man, middle aged, no you'd never guess if you met me! I came out to a few aged 27, went back in at 29, tried to live a 'normal' life, it didn't go very well, then aged 39 I came out again, finally got to the point where I thought, `I can't live like this anymore'... five years on and I've never been so well balanced before! Poetry happens when inspiration strikes, sometimes it's bad, sometimes it's good!

AJ (she/her): People misgender me because I sometimes dress in male clothes and sometimes female clothes, but my gender is male. I'm female to male (FTM). My male name is Sam but I'm not ready for people to call me that yet. I spend most of my time on an app called TikTok. I like creating short videos for people to watch and enjoy. I like painting, writing poems and writing songs so I can put my feelings and my thoughts and when I put it down it clears my head from everything that is going on in my head.

Ales Bear (he/him): I am an artist, author, blogger and trans man. Art and writing have always been my hiding spaces for when the world gets a little too loud. Most recently I have been blogging about being a trans man of the Druid faith, as well as tidbits of my journey. Poetry has always called to me, I was first published in anthologies as a teen, I'm just recently rediscovering my inner bard again.

Andi Mindel (they/them or she/her): The only thing I am sure of, in my post-menopausal, post-reproductive, post-sexual stage of life, is my heritage. My privilege, which I have to some degree deconstructed, holds me accountable by virtue of my education and my whiteness, marred only by my Jewish nose. I am a textile artist consumed by the notion of 'women's work' and semantics.

Ash Brockwell (he/him): I'm an artivist (that's not a typo, work It out!), a poet, a researcher, a project evaluation consultant, a teacher, a husband, a parent, and/or 'that queer bloke', depending who you ask. I co-founded Reconnecting Rainbows, a social enterprise promoting LGBTQIA+ mental wellbeing. Life truly did begin at 40 when I started my transition - coming out initially as non-binary, then transmasculine, and finally as a trans man in March 2018. When I'm not doing arty stuff, I love going on forest walks, watching *Star Trek* and spending time with my family.

Bingo Allison (they/them): I am an autistic, transfeminine, genderqueer person, and also an ordained curate in the Church of England. I am married with three small children. As well as moderating a Nonbinary Christians Tumblr blog and posting various poems, prayers, and stories for use by transgender and nonbinary people, I volunteer with the Chesterfield youth group run by Derbyshire LGBT+.

Devin Valentine (he/him): I used to write poetry as a young person, but over time lost the freedom to do so within myself for one reason or another. I recently had the opportunity to greet a storm coming in over the shore, and for the first time in years wrote some words in an artistic order.

Frogb0i (he/him): I am a trans man of colour currently based in Birmingham, UK. I like exploring nature, drawing, cooking, watching *Lord of the Rings* and playing with my two cats, Bilbo and Muffin. Find more of my work @g4rbagecat on Instagram.

Jani Franck (they/them): I am a nonbinary multidisciplinary artist working in visual art, land and site-specific installations, performance, music as well as poetry. I belong in the intertidal zone, the pause between beats, the spans of bridges and the edges of accepted reality. My art plays with symbol and ritual, blending the personal with the universal, exploring the links between ancient knowledge and where humanity is heading in these turbulent times. I embrace the liminal space of existing as bigender/genderfluid and the ability to walk between more than one set of different worlds.

Jon/Joan Knight (he/him): Born 1975 Jon Knight, I realised I was also Joan from the age of 4 onwards. I suppressed my female being from the age of 11 to 16 due to a homophobic climate at school, I carried on being Joan whenever I could in private. Then a close teacher friend helped me come to terms with who I was and Joan and Jon now share a genderfluid me. My wife and children have been beautifully supportive of us/me! I am a Quaker and a teacher and I truly hope that one day people will be judged solely on how they behave toward one another, not on gender, sexuality or sex.

Kay Whitehurst (she/her): I am Kay, a trans woman from the Midlands. I transitioned in 2018 and have been on the Nottingham list for 30 months at time of writing. Poetry has always been my go-to medium for relieving my dysphoria and depression and coping with my darkest thoughts and fears. Poetry flows for me, like water from a tap. It is my hope that I can convey to the reader a sense of my being, and so validate my own state of mind.

Kestral Gaian (she/her): I'm a writer and musician. I spend most of my time behind keyboards, both as part of legendary queer band Hunting Hearts and as a poet and novelist. My past works include COUNTERWEIGHTS, a collection of my early poetry, and HIDDEN LIVES, my debut teen drama novel.

Kim (they/them): I'm a multi-disciplinary artist who loves to write. I've been writing poetry and prose since my early teens and typically write pieces full of emotion.

Marcus Pabon-Lara (he/him): I am Deaf & proudly Colombian-born. My family moved to Britain when I was little. British Sign Language is my first & main language. During my teens, gaming, drawing and writing poems was my therapy for my temper. Importantly, writing the poems helped me in improving my English, and of course expanding my creativity and imagination ever more.

Megan Nightingale (she/her): I am trans* and ace, currently studying a degree in Sociology to later specialise in fields of understanding pertaining to gender identity, policy development and global inequality. I engage in activism circulating around the environment, LGBTQ+ rights and global development. Moreover, I volunteer for a number of charity organisations and serve as a panellist in equality committees across the UK, with my poetry exploring equality in different dimensions. I aspire to help all minority groups subject to discrimination on a global scale to enable them to gain access to further legal protections, social solidarity and appropriate support.

Paula Adrianne (she/her): I'm a 50-year-old pansexual trans woman, trying to stay safe and sane in a mad world set to self-destruct. I use poetry and activism to fight against bigotry and fascism, and have been rumoured to be the head of the Leeds trans mafia. I do all this whilst struggling with multiple life-threatening illnesses - my mantra is 'Don't dream it, be it'.

Queen Victoria Ortega (she/her): I'm a proud, brown and plus-size Latina. I believe in leadership through service. I am the CEO of Royalty Consulting Services and work alongside various NGOs to increase their capacity to work with people of Trans experience. I am also the President of FLUX, an organization based in the USA dedicated to creating content that promotes positive images of trans people. I leverage my intersectionality to advise and guide organizations and systems.

Rae-Lien Blais (they/them or he/him): I write and I use my words as an escape from explaining myself day-to-day. I have been a writer for many years. Writing has always been a huge part of my life as a living being. I am an artist as well as a certified Medical Assistant. I have always been better with my words rather than trying to just speak. Writing has taken the place of the anxiety my life creates. I do not conform to a gender - I am a conformer of {they/them/their}. My children call me 'he' for less confusion. I like to just be me, I am Rae. I am {Non-Binary}

The Refugee Trans Initiative is a non-profit, non-governmental organisation in Kenya that aims to ensure that refugee trans voices are heard and to create freedom and dignity for trans refugees. They have established a safe house for trans refugees who face eviction and mob violence and often fear for their lives. The three writers who have contributed to this anthology are Emily, Julie and Vanilla, who are among the founders of RTI and came to Kenya as refugees from Uganda and the Democratic Republic of the Congo.

RKP (they/them): I'm a gender queer drip artist, photographer and poet who doesn't shy away from exposing heartfelt raw words and nerves. Found at various Open Mics and Poetry events, born in the East and brought up in Cambridge, inspired by life & all things creative; I'm a colourful 'Jack of (almost nearly) all trades' and have been described as 'a pensive wordsmith who daringly invites the audience in to listen to their inspired "destructive yet fun" autobiographical poems'. For more info please see @RKP.PoetryAndPhotography on Facebook,

Samantha Smith (she/her): I'm a trans activist, sexual health volunteer, TDOR [Trans Day of Remembrance] organiser, and a police and equality LGBT panel member. I'm currently volunteering with Citizens' Advice as a witness support outreach worker. I work voluntarily supporting vulnerable and intimidated victims of crime. I will be holding a third consecutive vigil for TDOR in Leicester, United Kingdom. I'm also an animal rescuer and owner of my beloved posh dog.

The Bleeding Obvious (she/her): I'm a one-woman LGBT+ cabaret, currently heading into the realms of disco-funk as a prelude to my third album, *Dirty Blonde*. The second, *Rainbow Heart* (from which the lyrics included in this book are taken) led to a nationwide tour with dates in Bristol, York, Nottingham, Brighton, Leeds and Manchester, among others. I've played to a busy off-West End theatre for Pride In London and led a thousand-strong crowd in a singalong of *One Girl Girl* at Wakefield Pride. For someone who didn't want to do live shows, that's something of a turnaround! See www.thebleedingobvious.uk

Tina Cross (she/her or he/him): I am a gender fluid person - I am equally at home as male or female. I have become a bit of a minor celebrity in the trans community, appearing on Channel 4 and the BBC. Because of my confidence, others seem to trust me and I am a bit of an agony aunt to many girls with problems.

Tyler Richins (he/him): I'm 17 and new at poetry. I came out as trans a year ago. I live with my dad, who is not as open to me being trans as I would like. I was hoping *Letter To A Lost Girl* would help.

If you would like to contribute to the next Trans*(verse) poetry anthology, please e-mail transverse@ashbrockwell.com.

Trans*(verse) is supported by **Reconnecting Rainbows**, a UK social enterprise that promotes mental wellbeing within the LGBTQIA+ community. Reconnecting Rainbows provides bespoke training and consultancy at the intersection of diversity and workplace wellbeing, as well as signposting people to services and resources that can help them improve their mental health. It also runs the '#LIFEsaving Allies' online campaign to help people remember how to be better allies to their trans and non-binary friends:

L = Look at us as people

I = Identify us by the right names and pronouns

F = Find out what support we need today

E = Empower yourself to help us end transphobia!

For more information please visit www.reconnectingrainbows.co.uk

Lightning Source UK Ltd.
Milton Keynes UK
UKHW030758300819

348843UK00010B/787/P